A message to our Friends on Earth,

Report for duty immediately. Your Friends are waiting for you in Draco Sector. You are to undertake an important mission — the future of the Galaxy is in your hands!

Here are your instructions — prepare for action:

1. Start reading this book at once and discover what has been broken by the end of Chapter Two — this is your first password!

2. Log on to the Outernet by typing *www.go2outer.net* into your Internet browser, then enter this password to begin your adventure.

Once you have logged on, you will receive an o-mail from The Weaver explaining where to find your next password. There are passwords hidden in all the Outernet books. Every time you enter a password, remember to check your o-mails, FIB files, and Links carefully before moving on.

Good luck. You're going to need it.

Commander Huyu
Sector Commander, Draco Sector

Introducing something truly out of this world . . .

OUTERNET

WWW.GO2OUTER.NET

I: friend or foe?

II: control

control

Steve Barlow and Steve Skidmore

AN
APPLE
PAPERBACK

SCHOLASTIC INC.
New York Toronto London Auckland Sydney
Mexico City New Delhi Hong Kong Buenos Aires

To the memory of Douglas Adams

ISBN 0-439-34352-6

Published by Scholastic Inc., 557 Broadway, New York, NY 10012.
The Chicken House is published in the United States
in association with Scholastic.

12 11 10 9 8 7 6 5 4 3 2   3 4 5 6 7/0

Printed in the U.S.A.   40
First Scholastic printing, July 2002

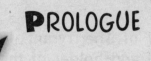PROLOGUE

Secret Headquarters of The Tyrant, the Forbidden Sector

The pyramid reared, dark and brooding, above the barren plain.

There are many pyramids in the Galaxy. On Earth, the Great Pyramid of the Egyptian Pharaoh Cheops is generally believed to be pretty impressive. Yet it pales into insignificance before the really Big Pyramid of Oompapus III on Monzeegus Prime.

And both of these structures, great though they are, would have been dwarfed by the Supercolossal Pyramid of Mewkus the Magnificent, Lord High Dribbler of the Slimethings of Squelch, if it hadn't unfortunately sunk into the fathomless swamp created by the disgusting secretions of the Slimethings themselves.

But even the Supercolossal Pyramid was of microscopic proportions when set against the

Dark Pyramid of The Tyrant, leader of the Forces of Evil and holder of the title "Most Foul, Wicked, and Depraved Being in the Galaxy" for ten gala-years running.

One of the claims advanced for the awesomeness of the Great Pyramid of Cheops is that it can be seen from outer space with the naked eye. But the Dark Pyramid is so huge that its peak is actually *in* outer space.

There are many theories to explain why pyramids exist on so many worlds. Some say that on Earth their dimensions are cunningly designed to mirror the positions of the stars. Others claim that they act as giant stone lenses to focus barely understood cosmic forces. Still others say they are just tombstones that got out of hand.

The truth of the matter is that pyramids are gateways to other dimensions. They allow beings to teleport from one part of the Galaxy to another without lots of tedious waiting around in spaceport lounges, followed by uncomfortable journeys in low-cost spaceliners, only to find upon arrival that their luggage is lost in a black hole. Plus, pyramids are easy to build and instantly recognizable. They are the interstellar equivalent of telephone booths — all the same shape (and often a little smelly).

However, the Dark Pyramid was to these lesser structures what AT&T was to two tin cans and a piece of string. As the fortress of the most evil being in the Galaxy, it was designed to be impregnable to all known forms of attack. A nuclear warhead wouldn't even dent it. A direct impact from an asteroid would be catastrophic, but only for the asteroid. The most powerful energy weapons might reduce the planet on which the pyramid sat to cinders, but the pyramid itself would remain unscathed.

Of course, in order to attack the pyramid, The Tyrant's few remaining enemies would first have to find it; and the planet on which it squatted, like an oversize cuckoo in a robin's nest, was carefully hidden among clouds of interstellar dust. It was also guarded by Detect-O-Matic alarm systems, FOEs patrol vessels, and self-propelling antiship mines to make sure that anyone who did find it would instantly wish they hadn't.

Inside the pyramid was probably the safest place in the Galaxy. And yet, there were at least two beings inside The Tyrant's headquarters who weren't feeling safe at all. This was because The Tyrant wanted to see them.

One of these beings was Tracer, The Tyrant's elephant-eared, virtual reality-visored chief of surveillance, who sat in the anteroom outside the presence chamber, nibbling, in a frenzy of anxiety, the claws on the end of every finger of its six manipulable limbs.

The other was the Big Bug, the leader of The Tyrant's most feared enforcers. Bugs are powerful, loyal, intelligent, and almost impervious to pain. It was that "almost" that was exercising the mind of the Big Bug as he waited to be shown into The Tyrant's inner sanctum. The Tyrant would almost certainly want the Big Bug to suffer and was known to enjoy a challenge.

At length, a door six feet thick slid open. Glancing nervously at each other, Tracer and the Big Bug stepped through.

They found themselves facing an elaborately carved screen from behind which came the scent of soft perfume and the sounds of sweet music. Beyond the screen, fountains tinkled and birds sang. But on the side where

4

Tracer and the Big Bug stood, there was only cold, bare steel. Lights shone on them in such a way that the figure behind the screen was invisible. The Tyrant never showed himself, even to his most favored allies. At the moment, Tracer and Big Bug weren't favored at all.

A low voice, cold as the space between the stars, echoed from behind the screen. "So there you are, my chief of surveillance."

Tracer instantly fell facedown to the floor, writhing in abject servility. "Greetings, O Great One. I grovel and abase myself before Your Awful Majesty."

"Very right and proper." The voice sent a chill to each of Tracer's three hearts. "Though whether it will save your miserable hide remains to be seen." The voice became chillier by several degrees. "And my head of security. What have you to say for yourself?"

The Big Bug could think of nothing to say that would improve its situation, so it said nothing.

"Let me remind you both," the evil voice continued, "of the outcome of your latest mission. You were entrusted with the task of securing the only Outernet Server not yet under my control. Would anyone like to tell me why this device is so important?" Three of Tracer's limbs instantly shot up and waved frantically to attract attention. "Yes?"

"So that you can control the entire Outer-net and use it for your own evil purposes, Your Appallingness."

"And I want to do this because . . . ?"

"Because then you can subject the whole Galaxy to a reign of terror and evil." Tracer looked smug.

"Very good. I'm glad you've read our mission statement. However, the miserable rabble of renegades and traitors who call themselves Friends continue to oppose my dreadful will. Yet in this instance, the Friends were totally at your mercy. The Server was located on a planet called . . . Dirt, or Soil, or some such thing. . . ."

"Earth, Your Atrociousness," Tracer cut in helpfully. "The planet's name is Earth."

The Tyrant's voice lashed out like wind-driven ice. "The planet's name will shortly be Mud, and so will yours if you ever presume to interrupt me again."

Tracer cringed. "I quail and cower before Your Evil Omnipotence."

"Yes, and you do it so well, too." For a moment, The Tyrant sounded grimly amused. "As I understand it," the voice continued, soft as the fall of snow on a tombstone, "you found The Server in the possession of primitive Earth-humans. Remind me what happened."

Tracer wrung all six hands. "I detected the humans on the pleasure planet of Arcadia, Your Malevolence. They returned to Earth by teleport, along with a native of Arcadia, a two-headed being of low intelligence and no consequence, who subsequently seems to have escaped. We must presume it is now hiding somewhere on Earth."

"And what of the humans?" prompted the icy voice.

"Two of them, Jack Armstrong and Lothar Gelt . . ."

"Lothar Gelt?" The Tyrant's voice was hardly more than a hiss. "One of the humans is called Lothar Gelt?"

"Yes, Your Vileness. And Jack Armstrong. Outlandish names, are they not?" Tracer gave an ingratiating cackle.

There was silence from behind the screen.

"I succeeded in capturing them," Tracer

continued hurriedly. "I interrogated them on your prison planet of Kazamblam."

"From which they subsequently escaped." The Tyrant's voice was icy with disapproval.

"They were allowed to get away, O Monstrous One. . . ." Tracer cowered. "It was all the Bug's idea!" The panic-stricken creature pointed accusingly at the Bug with two of his arms and buried his head in the other four.

The Big Bug stared at Tracer with furious contempt. "Sneak," it hissed. It raised its voice. "The escape was allowed, My Lord, so that the fleeing humans would lead my agent back to The Server."

"But your agent did not succeed in securing The Server," said The Tyrant in a low voice like the growling of a glacier grinding over naked rock. "Did it?"

"No, My Lord." The Big Bug shook its head uneasily.

"And now," said The Tyrant, "I believe the humans have used The Server to mobilize vast numbers of Links on Earth. Together, they have formed a Chain that renders our forces unable to teleport to Earth." The Tyrant sighed. "It's all terribly, terribly disappointing. What am I going to do with you?"

Trapdoors in the floor, walls, and ceiling swung open. Intense beams of force shot from each, enclosing the Big Bug in a cocoon of voracious energy.

"Oh, yes," said The Tyrant. "Now I remember."

Tracer scuttled into a corner, flattened his ears against his head, and hid his head in his hands, moaning and gibbering with fear.

When it was all over and the Big Bug was no more than a few wisps of greasy smoke hovering in the air, The Tyrant spoke again.

"Return to duty."

Tracer wiped the slobber from his chin and nodded quickly.

"I want The Server," The Tyrant continued. "You will get it for me. Whatever it takes. Do not fail me again, or your fate will make your colleague's seem merciful in comparison."

Tracer edged unsteadily toward the door.

"Oh, and send in the assistant head of security," said The Tyrant mildly. "I have good news for it. It's just been promoted."

CHAPTER ONE

3 The Almshouses, Little Slaughter, near Cambridge, England

It was Saturday. Decision day. Jack pulled himself out of bed with more reluctance than usual. It wasn't every day he was called upon to decide the future of the Galaxy.

He ran a hand through his dark hair, wiped the sleep from his eyes, and glanced down at the threadbare carpet where a small dog lay.

"Hi, Bitz," he said sleepily.

The dog responded with a tonguey yawn.

With his patchwork coat of wiry multi-colored hair, Bitz looked just like any other mongrel dog. However, in reality, Bitz was an alien life-form (an ALF). He was a chameleoid, a species that had the ability to change shape and form to blend into its surroundings. Upon his arrival on Earth, Bitz had taken the form of a dog.

More important, Bitz was an agent (code name Sirius) for the Friends Intelligence Bureau (FIB), an organization dedicated to defeating the Forces of Evil — the FOEs — and their leader, The Tyrant. Under the Friends agent's paws lay a black laptop computer — a fourteenth birthday present given to Jack by his parents only a few days earlier.

Like Bitz, the laptop wasn't what it seemed. It was The Server — an incredible piece of alien technology that allowed access to the Outernet. The whole system had been created by The Weaver for the free exchange of information between all advanced beings in the Galaxy.

Only the desperate action of Janus, Bitz's fellow Friends agent, had prevented The Server from falling into the hands of the FOEs. But in the struggle for The Server, Janus had been zapped into the nonexistence of N-space and was presumably dead. No wonder Bitz was looking subdued, his head down and his tail low.

Responsibility for looking after The Server now lay with the dog. It was a duty he took very seriously. However, Bitz had lost his ability to change shape. Stuck in his present canine form, Bitz needed the help of Jack and his human friends.

"We decide what to do today," said Jack grimly.

Bitz jumped up and gave a series of yaps and barks.

"Save your breath, you can't speak to me in English until I switch on The Server. Don't worry, it won't be long — we're meeting Loaf and Merle at the air base, then we'll decide what to do."

Jack threw on an old T-shirt and jeans. "Ready to go?" he asked as he bent down and picked up The Server. "Don't make noise — my mum and dad would have a fit if they knew I had a dog in my room."

Bitz nodded and followed Jack downstairs with his tail between his legs. Together they went out of the door, heading toward the American Air Force base and their destiny.

U.S. Air Force Base, Little Slaughter, near Cambridge, England

"Hey!" Loaf sauntered from the guardhouse at the entrance to the air base. Bitz, trotting at Jack's heel, gave Loaf an unfriendly look and made a noise in his throat that wasn't quite a growl.

Loaf ignored Bitz and held out a paper-wrapped package. "Happy birthday."

Jack gazed at him in astonishment — Loaf wasn't known for his generosity. In fact, it was very much the opposite. If there was a special Oscar category for "Best Display of Ego in a Selfish Role," Loaf would beat even the most self-centered Hollywood star hands down.

"It isn't my birthday," said Jack.

"So, I'm a few days late. Go ahead, open it."

Wordlessly, Jack obeyed. He opened the package and let out a low whistle. Loaf's present was a carrying case for a laptop computer. Bitz stood on his hind legs to get a closer look and gave an interrogative whine.

"Thought you'd better look after The Server properly. Happy birthday," repeated Loaf with a smile. Jack eyed him narrowly. Cheerful Loaf was as unfamiliar as generous Loaf. What was he up to?

Jack's look was misinterpreted by Loaf. "Don't worry, it's good quality. I have the same one." He patted another black case slung from his shoulder. "Dad got them for me."

Jack nodded knowingly. That made sense. Loaf's dad (Master Sergeant Carl Gelt) was the wheeler and dealer of the air force base. He could get ahold of anything (at a price) and would sell his own family if the money was good. Anyway, Loaf was right: The case was high quality. Jack pulled The Server out from under his arm and slipped it into the case as he mumbled his thanks.

"No problemo, amigo," smiled Loaf. "Let's go. I'll get authorization for you to come in." His friendly grin slipped a bit as he pointed at Bitz. "The alien dog has to sneak in."

Bitz gave a halfhearted snarl and slipped under the STOP barrier at the checkpoint. Loaf took Jack into the guardroom to sign him in. The little dog scampered to a nearby lamppost that provided cover and some interesting smells.

"Hi, Bitz!" The dog leaped up and barked joyously as Merle appeared. Her dark, pretty face broke into a beaming smile as she reached down and rubbed Bitz's ears. "Big day, huh?" She stood up and waited patiently for Loaf and Jack to pass through the security checkpoint.

"Hi, Jack," Merle waved.

Jack smiled and immediately wished he'd spent a few more minutes on his appearance. Merle's sense of style seemed to exaggerate Jack's "thrift shop" look (caused by his parents' lack of money). Even Loaf, with his baggy shirt, combat pants, and up-to-the-minute sneakers, put Jack to shame. "Hi, Merle," he said weakly.

Merle gave a grudging nod toward Loaf. "Let's head to my place." She turned and led the way toward her house.

The air force base was like a small American town stuck in the middle of England. There was housing for several thousand service personnel and their families, several schools, gyms, baseball fields, a Wal-Mart, a movie theater, bowling alley, and (perhaps most important for junk food enthusiasts like Loaf) *two* snack bars (as testified to by the size of Loaf's waistline).

"Your dad isn't home, is he?" Jack asked Merle. "We need to keep this discussion secret."

"Like we say in the air force — that's a negative," Merle told him. "There's some crisis or other, so he's out flying a mission. We won't be disturbed." As if on cue, two F-15 fighter planes screamed overhead, making Jack and Bitz flinch. Merle ignored the jets; as the base commander's daughter, she was used to the noise.

Merle paused on her doorstep and turned to Jack. "Do you have The Server?" Jack patted his new case. Merle looked at it and the identical case on Loaf's shoulder and raised her eyebrows. "Nice. Did Loaf's dad steal them?"

Loaf's grin slipped some more. "Do you know what slander is?"

"Yes, and I know how to spell it, which is more than you can do." Ignoring Loaf's scowl, Merle opened the door and stepped inside. Bitz padded in after her and directed a nod and growl toward the cat stretched out on the couch.

Like Bitz, Googie was a chameleoid. Unlike Bitz, she was not a Friends agent — quite the opposite. Googie (code name Vega) had once been an agent working for the FOEs.

Googie ignored Bitz's greeting and continued cleaning her blue-gray fur. Bitz shrugged and scratched at some of the many fleas that called his fur "home."

Jack carefully placed The Server's new

case on the table. "So, it's D day," he said. "What are we going to do about this? Janus gave us the choice: Return The Server to The Weaver or sit here and wait for the Friends to show up and take The Server back."

"Tough call," muttered Merle.

Jack nodded in agreement. "First things first. Do we turn on The Server?"

Merle pointed at Bitz and Googie. "Why don't we ask them? They're the alien experts."

Loaf snorted. "They can't talk to us until we switch on The Server, you dodo."

Merle's eyes narrowed. "If we ask them a question, they could bark or meow or nod their heads. They still understand us, Dodo," she added pointedly.

"Merle's right," said Jack, acting as peacemaker. He turned to Bitz and Googie. "Is it okay to switch on The Server?"

Googie gave an unconcerned meow. Bitz hesitated, then nodded.

Merle let out a whoop. "Alrighty, that's an affirmative. Let's log on."

On Jack's spoken command, The Server's lid clicked open, revealing a strange-looking keyboard with multisided keys.

Jack typed in *www.go2outer.net,* followed by his password and agent identity number. After a few seconds of static, the connection to the Outernet was made and luminous green letters flashed up on the screen.

Welcome, Friend.

The message was soon replaced by a desktop filled with various icons and a help button. One of the icons, an envelope surrounded by a circle, was flashing.

"Hey look!" Loaf pointed at the Outernet mail icon. "We've got o-mail — open it up."

"NO!" shouted Jack, Merle, Bitz, and Googie as one.

Loaf jumped back from The Server. "What's the matter?"

Merle jabbed a finger at his chest. "If you were any more stupid, you'd have to be watered twice a week."

Loaf's face became a mask of fury. "Good thing you're a girl. Or else . . ."

Merle thrust her face toward Loaf. "Yeah, good thing I *am* a girl, otherwise your stupid *boy* brain would have gotten us in major trouble."

"She's right," snarled Bitz. "At the moment, The Server is protected. All the Links being used by Friends on this planet are surrounding it with an impenetrable Chain. The minute you start receiving stuff from anywhere else in the Galaxy, the Chain will be broken. So you can switch on The Server, but that's all. No answering o-mails, no surfing the Outernet, and definitely no using t-mail to go teleporting!"

Loaf snorted. "That's dumb! Why can't we go surfing? We blocked the FOEs trace last time, didn't we?"

Bitz shook his head. "Hello?!! *I* stopped the trace, you mean. And believe me, where The Tyrant is concerned, you can't be too careful."

"Who wants to go teleporting?" Jack grimaced. "I don't want to end up being diverted back to Kazamblam." He had no happy memories of the time he, Loaf, and Googie had spent on The Tyrant's gloomy prison planet.

"I don't think that would happen," said Bitz reluctantly. "Even if the divert is still operating, we can bypass it now that we know it's there. But if we use the teleport function, we'll break the Chain — and then something else can teleport in and snatch The Server. We don't want any more Bugs down here. Janus isn't here to help us."

Loaf's customary scowl was back in place. "Okay, so what do we do?"

The discussion heated up. Bitz argued strongly that they should follow Janus's last request and return The Server to The Weaver.

Merle disagreed. "How do we do that? Janus said that no one knows who The Weaver is, so where do we go? And if we did go searching for The Weaver, how do we explain that to our parents?" She shook her head. "Can you imagine it? 'Sorry, Dad, I won't be home for dinner — I have to return a piece of alien technology to The Weaver, but I'm not sure who he or she is, where or even what he or she is, so I'm just going to teleport around the Galaxy. Don't wait up!' I'd be sent to the nearest shrink in seconds."

"Not a second too soon," sniped Loaf.

Merle ignored the wisecrack. "This whole thing is beyond us! It's not *Star Wars* or *The X-Files*. This is real! We should hand The Server over to the government. Let my dad have it. He'll know what to do."

Jack disagreed. "Janus didn't give us that option. He said if we didn't want to return The Server, we should wait for the Friends to send a ship to Earth to collect it."

"But the FOEs know The Server's here on Earth!" growled Bitz. "They're going to do exactly the same thing. Who says their ship won't get here sooner?"

Loaf gave a loud cough. "That's not the only choice."

"What do you mean?" asked Jack.

Loaf's eyes glinted. "Think about it. The Outernet is a fantastic opportunity. There are millions of sites out there and we haven't explored a fraction of them."

"What are you saying?" growled Bitz slowly.

"Just that we could make a killing! Send people on trips to planets. We could order alien goods and sell them to people on Earth. We could make a fortune!"

"The Outernet isn't yours to use like that!" Bitz protested.

"So whose is it?"

"No one owns it!" snapped Bitz. "The Outernet was created for the benefit of all life-forms in the Galaxy."

"Exactly!" exclaimed Loaf. "I'm a life-form and I'll benefit from making money!"

Merle shot Loaf a hard stare. "We need another opinion. What do you think, Googie?"

Googie flicked her whiskers. "I'm not being paid by Friends or FOEs, so I don't have a view. I just want to get off this dirt-ball planet as soon as possible."

"Oh, that's great!" Merle glared at Googie. "After all the time I've spent taking care of you."

"Sorry, human, but that's the way it goes. A few saucers of milk and bowls of foul-smelling cat food do not constitute grounds for a life-long friendship."

Merle turned her back on the cat. Jack patted her arm. "It's a tough call. I think we need Help."

There was a crackle of static, followed by a white light that burst out of The Server. It settled to reveal a holographic 3-D metallic head hovering above the keyboard. It was holding a paintbrush, which dripped virtual paint.

"Do you monkeys mind?" rasped Help, "I'm tryin' to decorate and I don't need you hasslin' me, if you would be so kind."

"Decorating?" asked Jack. "You're decorating a computer?"

"Yeah, decorating," snapped the hologram. "It's a mess in here. A mess caused by you primates letting a mad virus into my circuits! You should see it in here! Processors stripped bare, footprints all over the place."

"We need some help," demanded Loaf. "You're Help, so you've got to help us."

"Is that a fact, farm boy?" drawled Help. "Well, try this on for size: Kludge off!" In the blink of a cursor, the hologram disappeared back into The Server. In its place hung a sign:

Do NoT DiSTurb. EvEr.
(EsPEciAlly ThE MonkEy WiTh The uGly fAcE)

"Nice going, Loaf," said Merle wearily. "We need to argue this whole thing out rationally," she continued.

"Wrong!" Bitz growled. "There's no choice to make. Do what I say or I'll bite you in the leg."

"Oh, very rational!"

The room was instantly filled with personalities, opinions, and noise.

"We have to do what Janus said."

"Let's make some serious greenbacks. . . ."

"Give it to my dad. . . ."

The argument raged for some time. Finally, Jack held up his hand for silence. "Bitz, how long would it take the Friends to send a ship and pick up The Server?"

The dog shook his head. "Two — three weeks, minimum."

"All right. We wait. If no ship shows up in the next three weeks, we'll go looking for The Weaver."

"Putting off the decision again!" cried Merle.

Bitz pawed angrily at the ground. "You're making a big . . . *ruff, ruff. Grrr, wooof.*"

He was cut off midstream as Jack snapped The Server shut, put it in the carrying case, zipped it up, and placed it back on the table.

"*Aarrrowwwwlllll!*"

"What happens if the FOEs get here first?" demanded Merle.

"That's a chance we'll have to take," said Jack. "We're not trained agents. If we go shooting off across the Galaxy not knowing what we're doing or who we're looking for, we're more likely to get captured by the FOEs than we are to find The Weaver. Anyway, how

24

can we fight against The Tyrant? We're like ants to him. We've got no power!"

"So, give The Server to my dad," yelled Merle.

"Jack's right."

There was a silence as everyone turned to stare at Loaf.

"Did you just say that?" asked Jack.

"Yup," nodded Loaf. "The Server was your present, so it's your call." He handed Jack the carrying case and smiled. "Take good care of it. And no hard feelings."

Merle shook her head in disgust and Bitz howled in frustration.

3 The Almshouses, Little Slaughter, near Cambridge, England

Jack spent the rest of the day walking in the woods near the air base, thinking hard. Had he done the right thing? Or was Merle right? Was he just being indecisive? Bitz accompanied him on his walk, but Jack's halfhearted attempts to interest him in chasing sticks were met with stony looks. Bitz was sulking.

Jack arrived back at his house in time for a

silent supper with his mother and father. Bitz remained outside, lying low, waiting for Jack to sneak him back into the house.

"What have you been up to today?" ventured Jack's mom in an effort to start a conversation.

Jack shrugged. He couldn't tell his parents the truth. But he didn't like lying to them. "Not much," he answered. "Just been on the base with friends." (True.)

"Do anything interesting?"

"Not really." (Almost true — if you counted deciding the future of the Galaxy as being slightly boring.)

Jack's dad gave a grunt. "You spend too much time on that base, if you ask me. God knows, *I* do."

Jack tried to ignore his dad. These were not happy times. It had been different when they'd lived on the farm. But debts had mounted, forcing Jack's father to sell the farm, move, and find work with a contractor on the air force base.

The rest of the meal was eaten in silence. Jack was happy to finish his final spoonful of ice cream.

"Thanks, Mum." He jumped up from his chair and began to clear the dishes away.

As soon as he'd cleared the table and washed the dishes, Jack headed back to the sanctuary of his own room and flopped onto his bed. Questions spun in his head. Had he made the right decision? Should they wait until the Friends ship arrived? What if the FOEs got here first? Should he do what Bitz said? Why was this responsibility on his shoulders? Jack knew he was an insignificant human, just a minuscule part of a vast Galaxy full of life-forms he'd never imagined could have existed.

Jack stared at the carrying case and wondered whether Help would be in a more helpful mood. He picked up the case and began to unzip it. He reached in, pulled out the hard plastic casing — and gave a gasp of horror. The Server was gone and in its place was an ordinary laptop!

Jack began to rummage desperately through his memory for a clue. They'd used The Server . . . switched it off . . . put it back in the case. Then he'd picked it up and left.

No! Jack shook his head. He hadn't picked the case up — Loaf had handed it to him.

It must have been a mistake. Loaf had an identical carrying case — he'd obviously mixed them up. He wouldn't have done it on purpose, would he?

With a stomach-churning jolt of realization, Jack recalled Loaf's smile — it hadn't been a mistake.

Jack stared at the laptop he held in his hand. It was Loaf's.

Loaf had taken The Server.

CHAPTER TWO

U.S. Air Force Base, Little Slaughter, near Cambridge, England

Loaf gazed at the screen and rubbed his hands together.

"Oh, boy," he sang out happily. "Oh boy, oh boy, oh boy, oh boy, oh boy."

From the moment he'd first laid eyes on The Server, one thought had been at the front of Loaf's mind: How could he use it to make a profit? As far as he was concerned, the Galaxy could take care of itself. In any case, Jack and Merle were wimps. So maybe he'd put The Server at risk. Big deal. Business was all about taking risks, wasn't it? Get in quick, get out early, take the money, and run.

Loaf approved of business. Most of his associates (Loaf didn't have friends) had heroes who were film stars, sporting greats, or pop idols. All of Loaf's heroes were corporate high-fliers. Instead of actors, football players, and guitar legends, his bedroom walls were plastered with magazine photographs of very rich entrepreneurs. Men with smiles you could measure in kilowatts gazed down at Loaf approvingly as he chuckled over his find. Some wore snappy suits; others sported designer casuals and mirror shades as they waved to the camera from the decks of their private yachts. Loaf didn't think there was anything wrong with wealth, except that not enough of it belonged to him.

But all that was about to change. Loaf had just hit a gold mine.

He'd nearly given up, too, after several hours of wading through Outernet shopping sites full of stuff that nobody on Earth could possibly want. Loaf liked to think of himself as his father's son and prided himself on the fact that he could sell pretty much anything to anybody. But even he couldn't think of a way to make a profit selling alien cosmetics (green foundation, purple blush — *"For That Special Warty Look"* — or perfumes — *"Captivate Your Loved One with the Intoxicating Smell of Hydrogen Sulfide: It's the STYNX Effect!"*) to people on Earth.

Nor could he see much of a market for tentacle straighteners, antennae mufflers or geodesic spectacles for insectoid life-forms with compound eyes. And it was clear to him that there wouldn't be much demand for octophonic stereo headphones for creatures with four heads. Ditto on the things that looked like bulldozers with giant hands, which were apparently for huge swamp-dwelling lizards who got itches in places they couldn't reach to scratch.

But this was different.

Loaf gazed fondly at the screen and chuckled again as he read the advertisement for the umpteenth time:

Does Your Calculator Shut Off Halfway Through Solving a Crucial Problem?
Does Your 3-D Radio Break Up in the Middle of Your Favorite Song?
Does Your Holo-torch Give Out Just as You Reach the Darkest Corner of a Cave?
Does Your Atmospheric Skimmer Power Down at the Moment of Reentry?
Problem Solved!
Starburst Everlasting Batteries
Our Power Cells:

— Supply Any Level of Power
— To Any Appliance
— And Will NEVER Let You Down!
Only G$5.99 for a Pack of Three.
Order Today!

Loaf pulled a pad toward himself and began scribbling order details. He had no idea how much G$5.99 was in U.S. dollars, but it didn't sound like a fortune. Assume Galactibucks and dollars were worth about the same . . . and three batteries cost six dollars . . . that meant one would cost two dollars, and so if he ordered a thousand just to get started, that would cost . . . Loaf scribbled for a moment . . . two thousand dollars. Loaf grinned. He was sure his old man's credit card could stand that. And he could sell the batteries for at least five dollars apiece. That would net him five thousand dollars. After he'd paid his dad back, that was three thousand dollars clear profit!

There were a few other items — Galactic Added Tax, Postage, and Packing. Chickenfeed. Loaf moved the screen pointer to the ORDER button and clicked on it decisively.

* * *

Merle's cell phone buzzed. She made a dive for it, but her father got there first.

"You're not going out tonight."

"Dad! Do you mind?"

Colonel Frank Stone held the phone at arm's length away from Merle. "You have work to do, young lady. You've already missed three assignments this semester."

"Okay, I hear you! Now may I please take *my* call? On *my* phone?"

Grudgingly, Colonel Stone handed the phone over. Merle snatched at it and left the room with a determined stride.

With a sigh, Colonel Stone returned to his papers. After a few moments, he looked up to see Major Jackson grinning at him.

"You got any comments to make, Hal?"

His aide's grin broadened. "Not a word, Colonel."

Colonel Stone shook his head. "I swear, Hal, I don't know what to do with that girl. I suppose you think I should cut her some slack."

Hal Jackson shrugged. "Not for me to say, Frank. She's a good kid."

"I guess." Colonel Stone stared into space. "A girl that age needs her mother."

Major Jackson said nothing. Merle's mother had died in a car accident three years before. That wasn't the colonel's fault. Dependents of military personnel had a tough life. That wasn't the colonel's fault, either. Merle was pretty well-adjusted, considering, but that didn't stop Frank Stone from wondering whether he was a bad father.

Colonel Stone shook his head over the papers. "I need some figures from the office to make sense of this stuff."

Major Jackson raised his eyebrows. "Isn't it a little late to be going back to your desk?" He caught his commanding officer's frown and dragged himself out of his armchair. "I'll walk across to Wing HQ with you."

In her room, Merle batted Googie off the couch. The cat gave her an I-was-just-getting-up-anyway look and started to wash herself. Merle flopped onto the couch and answered the phone.

"Merle?" Jack's worried voice crackled in

her ear. She could hear Bitz yapping frantically in the background.

"Jack? What's up?"

"Shut up, you stupid dog!" Jack's voice faded as he yelled at Bitz. His voice became clear again. "Loaf's got The Server."

"What?" Merle sat bolt upright. "You gave Loaf The Server? Are you crazy?" Googie leaped up, ears back, tail bristling.

Jack snorted. "I didn't say I gave it to him. I said he's got it. He must have switched cases on me this afternoon."

"Well, go get it back!"

"I can't!" Jack's voice was harsh with frustration. "I can't come onto the base without permission. You know that."

Merle said a word that wasn't at all suitable for the daughter of a colonel in the U.S. Air Force. "Okay. Meet me at the gate. We'll find him together." Merle broke the connection and thought furiously. Loaf must be planning to use The Server. But what for? She punched a pillow. This was no time for guessing. They'd find Loaf, they'd find out what he was up to, then they'd beat him up. No, they'd beat him up, *then* they'd find out what he was up to.

Merle poked her head out of her room just in time to see her father and Major Jackson go out the front door. Great! Dad going out will make this a lot easier. Merle scurried upstairs and made a fake body in her bed with pillows and blankets. Then she grabbed a denim jacket and hurried out into the night. Googie streaked ahead.

Loaf frowned at the screen. He'd tried ordering the Everlasting Batteries, but Starburst Inc. wouldn't accept his dad's credit card details. He'd tried various galactic banks, but none of them had been willing to give him a loan. Finally, he'd found a credit company called *Twista, Grifta, Sharpie & Bent*. They hadn't bothered with too many credit checks — in fact, they'd been falling over themselves to lend him money at what seemed to be an incredibly low interest rate. So Loaf had agreed to the loan contract, given them his dad's credit card details, and ordered the batteries, which were scheduled for immediate rush delivery by t-mail.

Loaf felt very smug for about thirty seconds. Then he started worrying. It all seemed just a little too easy. Had he missed something?

He called Help.

The silver-gray hologram materialized in its customary place above The Server's keyboard and responded with its usual lack of charm. "Whaddaya want, primate? And it better be good."

"I need some financial advice."

"You got it, cheesehead!" Instantly, the hologram popped on a visor with a green eyeshade. "You're lookin' at the smoothest operator in the sector. You wanna carve a slice, you've come to the right application, kiddo."

Loaf told Help about the batteries.

"What'd they cost you?"

"Just under two thousand Galactibucks. What's that in dollars?"

Help's eyes rotated as it did the conversion. "About thirty million."

"What?"

"Good price."

"What?"

"Everlasting batteries are expensive. Why

do you think nobody bothers with them? You can buy about a billion conventional batteries for the price of one everlasting cell, which is only gonna pay for itself after you're long dead."

Loaf suddenly felt the need to sit down. "Plus G.A.T.," he added weakly.

"*Plus* Galactic Added Tax? Oh, boy."

Loaf had a bad feeling about what was coming next, but he had to ask. "How much is G.A.T.?"

Help was clearly enjoying itself. "Last I heard, four thousand percent."

Loaf could only gape.

"'Course," Help went on, "I've been stuck on this kludgy little planet for some time now. It may have gone up. It takes a whole heap of taxes to run a Galaxy."

"Wuk," agreed Loaf, his eyeballs threatening to pop.

"Tell me," said Help, with a casual leer. "Did they sting you for postage as well?"

Loaf nodded wordlessly.

Help threw back its head and cackled.

"Aha-ha-ha-ha-ha-ha-ha-ha-ha-ha-ha-ha-ha-ha!"

Loaf ran a finger around his collar. "How much," he said hoarsely, "do you think that might be?"

"Well," said Help judiciously. "The factory is on the other side of the Galaxy, and they'll have to route it around the central lens — too many black holes, they really kludge up teleportation — let's see . . . call it another ten million."

Loaf dived for his pad and scribbled. "That's . . ." He made a ghastly rattling noise at the back of his throat and stammered, "That adds up to a hundred and thirty million dollars." He reached for the keyboard. "I'll cancel the order!"

"No chance." Help shook its metallic head and gave Loaf an evil grin. "Galactic contract law. Once an agreement's made, that's it."

"But I borrowed the money!" Loaf screamed. "Off Twista, Grifta, Sharpie & Bent."

"Those sharks?" Help's grin got even wider. "I'll send flowers."

"At three percent per standard galactic year." Loaf moistened his lips and asked, "How long is a standard galactic year?"

"You won't like it."

"Just tell me."

"About twenty Earth minutes. You're gonna lose legs, fella. How many you got?"

"Two."

Help cackled. "Not enough. I once knew a Munervian millipede who took a loan he couldn't afford. Now he don't walk so good. Last time I saw him he was a quadruped."

Loaf stared wild-eyed at Help. "What am I going to do?"

"Die with dignity. Uh-oh, incoming traffic. Gotta go."

The hologram faded. The screen lit up with a message.

Receiving teleport.

Loaf slumped at his desk and hid his face in his hands, which was a pity, because he missed the arrival of a large wooden box by t-mail. It was quite impressive.

However, Merle and Jack, with Googie and Bitz at their heels, burst into Loaf's room just in time to catch the show. A chill, biting wind from half a galaxy away sent loose papers whirling and curtains flapping. The walls of Loaf's bedroom flashed in blue-white light that skittered across the walls and arced into the center of the room. Loaf's delivery slowly materialized between the foot of the bed and the closet.

Jack shielded his eyes from the glare. When the light faded, he blinked and made a lunge. He hauled Loaf to his feet. "What have you done?"

Bitz snarled. "Later! We've got to shut that thing down, quick."

Merle grabbed The Server. A message was flashing on the screen as she pounded frantically at the keys.

Your order has arrived.

"Howdy, y'all!" The message had disappeared, replaced by a blue-green alien that grinned happily and waved at them. "You get a special free gift fer orderin' within thirty days. Guess who."

"Virus!" spat Googie. "It must have backpacked on the teleport signal."

"It did." A deep, muffled voice sounded from inside the wooden box. "So did I."

The packing crate splintered as something massive smashed its way out. The occupant of the crate shrugged off shards of packaging and rose up until it almost filled the room.

Loaf wailed. "Hey! What happened to my batteries?"

Merle stood, paralyzed with shock. Bitz whined and backed away. Googie wriggled backward under the bed, hissing. Jack let go of Loaf, who fell to his knees, and let out a despairing groan. "Bug!"

The Chain had been broken. Their enemies were upon them. Earth lay wide open to the forces of The Tyrant.

CHAPTER THREE

"Gimme The Server," snapped Bitz. "Quick!"

Merle hesitated for a fraction of a second, then snapped the laptop shut and held it out to Bitz. The dog snatched The Server in his jaws, darted between the surprised Bug's legs, and raced out of the room. The Bug roared in anger and frustration. Ignoring the others, it lumbered around and stampeded in pursuit of Bitz. The walls shook.

Jack grabbed Merle's sleeve. "Come on! Bitz can't carry anything that heavy for long. He'll need our help." He turned to Loaf. "Let's go!"

"Leave me out of this!" Loaf's face was pale. "I've had a bad day."

Merle hauled him to his feet. "It's going to get worse." She and Jack dragged Loaf from the room, through the house, and out onto the driveway. Googie padded along behind.

At this time in the evening, the living quarters on the base were quiet. The street was almost deserted. Jack gave a groan. "Which way?"

Merle scanned the sidewalks and spotted an airman some distance away, staring blankly into space. A paper sack of spilled groceries lay at his feet. Merle sprinted across to him.

The airman turned haunted eyes on her. "Did I just see a rhinoceros in a three-piece suit come through here chasing a dog with a computer in its mouth?"

"No," answered Merle.

"Oh. Good."

"Which way did they go?"

"Who?"

"The dog and the rhinoceros you definitely didn't see. Which way did they go?"

Speechless, the man pointed.

"Thank you." Merle sped away, pursued by Jack and Loaf.

The airman watched them go. "You're welcome."

Three blocks away, Loaf, Jack, and Merle came to a halt, panting. Googie leaped onto a wall, then a garage, and finally onto a house roof, where she sat staring into the night.

Merle gave Loaf a very unfriendly look. "If we survive this, I'm going to kill you."

"Hey, it wasn't my fault!" Loaf looked at Merle and Jack and realized that he wasn't in a very good position. "Okay, so maybe it was. Geez, I was just tryin' to make an honest buck. . . ."

"Honest!" Merle laughed bitterly.

"Well, how was I supposed to know Bug was gonna show up? I thought we got rid of it!"

"Janus got rid of *a* Bug," Merle corrected. "Bitz told us Bugs were The Tyrant's hired muscle, remember? They're a whole species."

"But this one looks just like the other one."

"Like you'd know one Bug from another. We don't have time for this! Where's Bitz?"

From her rooftop, Googie yowled, then sped down to join them. Moments later, Bitz appeared in the glow from a distant street-light. He was running. His body was low to the ground, his head up, to keep The Server from

45

dragging on the street. His ears were back, his short legs almost a blur. He had reason to hurry. The Bug came around the corner behind him, pounding along at a full charge.

"Uh-oh." Loaf took off. Googie followed. Merle gave Jack a shove. "Go ahead. Make for the football field. I've got a plan."

Jack nodded and ran. Merle waited until Bitz caught up with her. She snatched The Server and backed away as the Bug rushed toward her.

Merle waited until the Bug was almost upon her before sidestepping with a neat salsa body swerve. The Bug plunged past her and clattered into a cluster of garbage cans by the side of the road. By the time the furious creature had removed itself from a collection of empty cans and fish heads, Merle and Bitz had a good head start. With a roar, the Bug lumbered behind them in pursuit.

Loaf, Jack, and Googie tore onto the floodlit field where the base football team was in the middle of a practice session. Jack skidded to a halt behind a defensive formation just as Merle and Bitz, with the Bug in pursuit, appeared on the other side of the human wall.

Jack groaned. He'd never get to Merle in time — there were too many bodies in the way.

Merle didn't hesitate. She raced toward the team captain. "Hey, Ken! This guy's chasing me!"

"Yeah?" Ken stared across the floodlit field, screwing his eyes up against the dazzle of the lights. The Bug's size didn't phase him. Any guy who needed that much body armor had to be a pussycat. Ken dropped into a crouch. "Listen up, team!" he roared. "Twenty-four . . . forty-eight . . . seven . . . er . . . ah, the heck with it! Just take him out, you guys!"

Twenty-two feet churned the dried dirt of the field. Merle swung her arm back and hurled The Server in a long upfield pass. It spun over the defensive line into Jack's waiting hands. Just as the Bug reached Merle, it was astonished to find itself the target of an avalanche of armored bodies.

By the time the Bug had freed itself, Jack and Merle had disappeared.

In an unlit corner behind the sports center, Loaf leaned against a wall and sucked in air in

great wheezing gasps. Bitz lay with paws out-
stretched and tongue lolling. Merle, trying to
catch her breath, opened the lid of the laptop.

Immediately, Help materialized, staring
around wildly. "Ow! Ooh! Hey, will you
kludges quit stallin' and do somethin'? Get
this guy outta my memory!" The hologram
flickered and disappeared again.

Virus appeared on the screen, wearing a
Davy Crockett hat and carrying a rifle. The
electronic life-form turned to look out of the
screen. It held a finger to its lips. "Sssshhhh!
Be werry, werry quiet. I'm hunting wabbits." It
winked at its audience and moved offscreen
on tiptoe.

Googie (the only one who seemed not to
be out of breath) hissed, "You've got to get
that thing out of there before it's too late."

"Hey!" Loaf looked up for just long enough
to gasp, "The furball's talking again!"

"Because The Server's on, dum-dum."
Merle turned to the cat. "Why do we have to
get it out, Googie?"

"It's trying to access The Server's memory.
If it succeeds, it can download all the Friends
secret files straight to The Tyrant."

"So what?" sneered Loaf.

"So, The Tyrant will know the names and identities of every Friends agent in the Galaxy," spat Googie. "He'll also get my details, and if that happens, I will personally tear you to pieces."

"Oh, yeah?" challenged Loaf.

Googie's eyes narrowed. "I'm a chameleoid, remember? I can turn into creatures that would give your *nightmares* nightmares. Do you want to meet a Bogian Butt-chewer? A Xeronian Gut-guzzler? An Eyeball-popping Razor-toothed Ear-driller from the planet Aaaaaargh? Just say the word."

Loaf shifted uncomfortably. "The planet Argh?"

"Aaaaaargh. Six *a*'s. That's what visitors call it — it's the first word they say on arriving. It's also their *last* word."

"You're just trying to scare me," blustered Loaf. "You can't change form anymore. Bitz said so."

Googie stretched and unsheathed her claws. "Bet your life?"

Loaf said nothing. Help appeared again, hologrammatic eyeballs rotating at high speed in opposite directions. "Help! He's picking my brains, here!"

Jack drew in a shuddering breath. "We've got to keep moving."

Merle shook her head stubbornly. "There's no point in just running around like headless chickens. The Bug would catch us sooner or later. We've got to figure out what to do." She began tapping the computer keys.

Jack bent closer. "What are you doing?"

"I was watching when Janus typed in the sequence that got rid of Virus the first time. I'm trying to remember it. . . ." She tapped several more keys.

Virus reappeared on the screen. "Close," he told Merle, "but not close enough." The virtual nuisance chuckled and looked around. "Where are you, you wascally wabbit?" It disappeared again.

Help appeared, screeching like a train whistle. Hologrammatic steam poured from its ears. "Do something!" it gurgled.

Muttering rude words under her breath, Merle tried another sequence. Bitz staggered to his feet and tottered over.

Merle clenched her fists in frustration. "What did Janus *do*?"

Help was tarnishing. Its metallic sheen was being eaten away by rust, and green goo was dribbling from its seams. It made a supreme effort to speak. "This creep's corrupting my memory," it wheezed. "So what you kludges gotta do is, you gotta initiate the antivirus software . . . geeble wibble twok, an error of type Oh, Ma Darlin' Clementine has occurred, shut down all Doo Wah Diddy Diddy Dum Diddy Doos and restart your Way down upon the Swanee River — Take your partner, do-si-do . . ."

Bitz yapped triumphantly. "Antivirus software — that's what Janus was doing."

"Antivirus software . . . antivirus software . . ." Merle's eyes opened wide as enlightenment struck. "Omigosh — *antivirus software*!" She tapped furiously at the keys.

Virus reappeared on the screen. Its image began to break up. A look of fury appeared on its pixeled face before the image exploded. A million dots of light seethed briefly across the screen before swirling into a whirlpool of color that drained away to nothing. Virus's voice floated to them, fading into distance; "Oooooooh, I hate that wabbit. . . ."

Help reappeared, looking very much the worse for wear. "Kludge! Take your time, why don't you?" It started to fade. "If anybody wants me, tough. I'm going into rehab." The hologram disappeared. A message appeared on the screen:

> *Antivirus software is now*
> *repairing corrupted files.*
> *Please stand by.*

Jack gave a sigh of relief. "Well, that seemed to work. What were you typing in before?"

"'Open Aunty Ivy's sock drawer,'" Merle muttered.

Jack stared at her, openmouthed. "Aunty Ivy's *sock drawer*?"

"I thought it was a code," snapped Merle defensively. "It *looked* like 'Aunty Ivy's sock drawer'."

Jack shook his head.

"Whatever," said Loaf, casting nervous glances all around. "We may have gotten rid of Virus, but that Bug is still after us."

"And whose fault is that?" demanded Bitz.

"Go chase a stick." Loaf turned to Jack and Merle. "Come on — let's keep running."

"No point," barked Bitz. "We can't outrun it forever."

"Let's start with the next ten minutes," said Loaf, "and worry about 'forever' later."

"No," Jack said forcefully. "The FOEs are here. There's no point in waiting for the Friends. It's decision time — and it's up to us now. We have to get out there and find The Weaver."

"About time!" yapped Bitz.

Loaf scowled. "So where do we start?"

"Anywhere that's not here!" Bitz turned to Merle. "The coordinates for the planet Arcadia are still in The Server's memory. You'll need to select SELF TELEPORT to take The Server with you. Then press SEND," Bitz continued, "and you'll get away."

"Us?" Jack's voice was tense. "What about you?"

"*Rrrrrrroooowwwwww!*" Googie's caterwaul cut off Bitz's reply and brought them all to their feet. They turned to see the Bug silhouetted in the beam of a security light several buildings away. At the same moment, the Bug spotted

its prey. Its shoulders hunched. Like a loco-
motive gathering speed, it lumbered toward
them, moving from rest to a jog, a canter, a gal-
lop, and finally to a full charge. Merle took one
look at it and began tapping keys.

"Janus sent a rescue mission to Earth to re-
cover The Server," said Bitz hurriedly. "Someone has to stay around and tell them what
happened, and keep an eye on the big fella."
Bitz jerked his head at the approaching Bug,
who was almost upon them.

Googie leaped onto Merle's shoulder. "I'm
with you."

"Ow!" Merle made a face but kept punch-
ing keys. "Watch those claws, okay?" She
looked up. "Got it." Her finger hovered over
the SEND key. "Ready?"

Bitz danced to one side. "Do it!"

Merle hit the key. She, Jack, Loaf, and Googie were outlined in flares of blue-white light.
They dematerialized and disappeared.

A fraction of a second later, the Bug, unable
to stop, charged through the empty air where
they had stood and crashed full tilt into the
solid brick wall of the sports center.

The wall exploded inward. The Bug found

itself lying amid a pile of bricks and a cloud of dust. It shook its head irritably and sneezed.

It clambered out through the hole it had made. Bitz, the chameleoid agent of the Friends, had already disappeared. There were distant shouts. Time for the Bug to make itself scarce. It shook its head unhappily. The Tyrant was NOT going to be pleased.

CHAPTER FOUR

Unknown Planet, Draco Sector

Jack still wasn't sold on teleportation as a means of travel. True, it could send him to distant planets in the blink of an eye, but there was a big downside. It gave him motion sickness with attitude.

As Merle hit the SEND button, Jack's molecules were broken down, one by one. He felt like a tomato in a blender. After an incomprehensible period of time (a second? a year? an ice age?), the sensation reversed — like a movie played backward. Jack felt his organs spin back into place and his skin close up over them. With a final thundering jolt to the senses, consciousness returned.

Jack blinked, shook his head groggily, and looked around. Merle, Loaf, and Googie stood by his side. They were all rocking unsteadily on their feet. And staring wide-eyed . . .

"I don't remember Arcadia looking like this," said Merle slowly. "Where are the crowds? Where are the rides?"

They gazed around at the barren landscape that surrounded them. They seemed to be standing in the middle of a vast desert, made up of hard-baked earth covered with a film of red dust, with sharp, jagged stones jutting through it.

Craters and small hills added to the ominous lunarlike surroundings. Light from three dull moons tried desperately to pierce the oppressive atmosphere. The silence was palpable. Even the small gusts of wind that whipped up the dust around their feet were silent. The cold air bit into their bones.

"Maybe it's a part of Arcadia we didn't see before," suggested Jack unconvincingly.

"I don't see Mr. Tickly Wickly," said Loaf, recalling the annoying Arcadian theme park host.

In the distance, there were huge red sandstone cliffs that climbed up into the deep maroon sky. Below them lay something that might have been described as a city — by someone who wasn't too picky about definitions. It was a collection of incredibly ugly structures that didn't look "built" so much as "dropped," as if the inhabitants of several spectacularly messy star systems had dumped their garbage over the cliffs and the locals had simply moved into the debris.

Googie looked up at Merle. "You did hit the correct destination, didn't you?"

Merle raised an eyebrow. "It said Arcadia, I hit Arcadia. We should be on Arcadia."

The Server pinged. A message appeared on the screen.

Antivirus self-repair program complete.
Your Server will now function normally.

Googie yowled. "If The Server only just finished repairing itself, then its memory was still corrupted when we teleported off Earth. We thought it would send us to Arcadia because those coordinates were in its memory, but . . ."

"But if its memory was corrupted, the coordinates were probably wrong." Merle groaned. "That explains why we've landed here."

Jack looked around at the desolation. "Wherever 'here' is." He took The Server from Merle's hand. "Let's get some Help."

The hologram appeared in the blink of a cursor. "What now?!" Help snapped. "Are you bozos planning to mess up my head again?"

The others looked quizzically at the metallic head.

"You let in the Virus!" Help bobbed up and down angrily. "I had barely finished cleaning up after its first visit and you let it in again! Why are you torturing me? Is there a reason for this, or are you just plain STUPID?!" Help's eyes suddenly narrowed suspiciously. "Just a minute — where am I? Where did you dumb monkeys bring me to now?"

Jack shrugged. "We were hoping you could tell us."

"Sheesh!" The hologram's eyes spun wildly. "Work, work, work! Okay, lemme run some tests." It muttered to itself for a few moments. "Landscape . . . spectral analysis of light . . . atmosphere . . . scanning for minerals . . . cross-referencing data files . . ." Help's hologrammatic eyes suddenly widened. "Uh-oh." The hologram gulped. "We appear to be on planet Deadrock, Draco Sector, thank you for using Help, good-bye. . . ." The hologram shot back into the safety of The Server. In its place hung a sign:

GoNE AwAy — baCk iN a MillENniuM or TwO.

"Deadrock? Oh, no . . ." Googie gave a yowl of alarm. "That's bad. It's worse than bad. Think bad, put it in capital letters, cube it, and add several hundred zeros and you'll still not be close to how bad Deadrock is."

Jack sighed. "What's so bad about it?"

"Nobody knows exactly," admitted Googie, "because nobody who's visited Deadrock has ever come back."

Loaf indicated The Server. "Why don't we go on-line and find out more about Deadrock?"

His suggestion was met with howls from Googie.

"We'll give away our location again," Merle noted.

"We could still use The Server. . . ." Googie cut in. "Help recognized the planet, so it must have data on it somewhere in its memory. You won't have to go on-line to access that. The

Friends Intelligence Bureau has information on all inhabited planets. There's probably an FIB file on Deadrock."

Googie was right. There was.

Merle grinned as the file flashed up on screen and the others crouched around. "Let's see what it says." Her smile quickly disappeared.

Googie was right again. It *was* bad.

Loaf read the entry apprehensively. "The local life-forms sound like bad news. Does anybody know what Nawgaws are?"

"Never mind the local life-forms," growled Googie. "The whole planet is obviously crawling with FOEs."

Merle wrinkled her nose. "Check out the weather. Doesn't sound like the sort of place you'd want to build a resort. Or spend the night, come to think of it."

Jack pointed toward the ramshackle settlement under the cliffs. "If that's A'void City, the capital," he said, "it's well named. We couldn't have picked a much worse planet to visit if we'd been trying." He sighed. "Oh, well, The Server's working now. All we have to do is input some new coordinates and teleport out of here."

"Good idea, Jack." Merle's voice was quiet and rather flat. "Unfortunately, I think we have a problem."

She turned The Server's screen so that Jack and Loaf could read the message that was flashing urgently in the center:

Low battery power.
T-mail disabled.

Googie read the message and groaned. "That klutz of a dog probably hasn't recharged the batteries since he got to Earth."

Jack stared at the screen in dismay. "Is The Server going to shut down?"

"No. Most of its functions don't use much power. But a teleportation event takes an awful lot of energy. I'm afraid we're stuck here on Deadrock until we can find a way to recharge it." Googie began to walk up the small hill. "We can't just sit out here in the desert. We're lucky we arrived in the evening. If we stay out in the open, we'll either freeze tonight or burn to death tomorrow. We don't have a choice — there's just no way we can avoid A'void."

Jack nodded. "Googie's right. We'll head toward the cliffs."

Googie turned and padded on. Jack and Loaf exchanged glances and followed the cat. Merle gazed apprehensively at the city, then up at the frozen moons. A chill wind streamed silently past her. Merle pulled her jacket tighter and hurried after the others.

None of them saw the red-robed figure who stood in the shadow of a jagged rock, watching them go.

U.S. Air Force Base, Little Slaughter, near Cambridge, England

Back on Earth, an alien with the size, skin tone, and disposition of a rhinoceros was muttering at its watch.

The Bug was trying to contact Tracer, The Tyrant's chief of surveillance operations, via the small communications device it wore on its forearm. This was difficult to see because it blended into the Bug's body and looked like just another muscle (of which the Bug had plenty).

As it muttered, the Bug punched in the dialing coordinates for Kazamblam, communications center for the FOEs. Then it sat back and waited apprehensively.

Seconds later, the small screen crackled into life and a head with large ears and a VR visor appeared. The Bug breathed deeply and began to relate its tale of failure to Tracer.

"Oh dear, oh dear, oh dear." Tracer's visor pulsed with sparks of colored light as he shook his head. "His Wickedness is going to be incredibly underwhelmed with you."

The Bug winced. It had heard stories of The Tyrant's wrath and knew the price of failure. One of the Evil Lord's many mantras was printed on the front page of every Bug training manual:

> IF AT FIRST YOU DON'T SUCCEED, YOU WILL BE
> PUNISHED IN TERRIFYING AND HORRIFIC WAYS.

"I can get The Server back," insisted the Bug in its surprisingly cultured voice. "All I need is some backup."

The VR visor flashed violently. "Backup? Hmmm. I'll have to get authorization." Tracer paused. "From the very Highest Authority." He didn't look happy at the prospect.

The Bug broke out in a cold sweat. It reached into its pocket and took out a handkerchief (made from the best Saluvian silk). It patted its low, furrowed brow as it tried to make out the conversation taking place many thousands of light-years away.

Tracer's side of his conversation with The Tyrant wafted to the Bug's ears. "Yes, Your Terrible Omnipotence . . . escaped by teleport . . . yes, very unfortunate Your Despotic Greatness. . . . No, it doesn't know where they are. . . . Yes, it would look extremely good as a floor covering. . . ." (The Bug winced.) "And would be of more use . . . ha-ha-ha." (The Bug winced even more.) "It is requesting backup. . . . No, Your Glorious Nastiness . . . no, I quite understand, Your Malign Majesty. . . . Yes, yes, thank you, O Evil One."

The Bug stared expectantly at the screen as Tracer turned back, VR visor twinkling.

"There. That was a very successful outcome."

The Bug looked relieved. It was somewhat premature.

"Of course, His Appalling Highness has refused to sanction any backup. He feels that you, as one of his chief enforcers, who have brought fear and trepidation to the farthest reaches of the Galaxy, should have the where-withal to defeat these pathetic subspecies and return The Server immediately. He also wishes to remind you that there is an unending sup-ply of Bugs like you, and therefore you are ex-pendable."

The Bug began patting its brow again. "So in what way was that a successful outcome?" it asked mournfully.

Tracer gave a playful laugh. "Because he's not blaming me!"

The Bug rubbed at its piggy eyes. "But what am I supposed to do? I don't know where the Earthlings have taken The Server. Help me, please."

Normally, Tracer would have let the Bug stew (as it surely would when it returned to Kazamblam, possibly prior to being eaten), but this situation was different. The Tyrant de-manded results, and if the Bug failed, Tracer would also suffer The Tyrant's wrath.

"All right. Since you asked so nicely . . ." The VR visor glowed bright red, "This is what you're going to do. . . ."

Hidden behind a nearby hedge as the Bug repeated its instructions, Bitz listened and shivered.

A'void City, Planet Deadrock, Draco Sector

A'void City was living up to its name. All the alien life-forms that walked, slithered, hovered, and bounced down the walkways and skyways of Deadrock's only metropolis were doing their best to avoid any contact with the newly arrived visitors.

Any form of greeting the three humans attempted was shunned. Waves, smiles, and nods of the head received no response, and when Jack shouted a breezy hello to a small, furry alien, the creature scuttled away as fast as its teddy-bearlike legs could carry it.

"Not very friendly," muttered Merle.

All around was the bustle of a city. Under blazing streetlights, aliens of all shapes, sizes, and colors made their way into and out of stores and restaurants. But there was something wrong, something missing. Merle was the first to spot it.

"Nobody is talking."

It was true. The city mirrored the silence of the desert.

"And another thing," warned Googie. "We're being watched." She nodded skyward. The others followed her glance. Small cameras, fixed to the sides and roof of every building, seemed to be pointing at them.

The camera eyes silently turned and followed the visitors as they rounded a corner and came into a plaza, bordered on one side by a forbidding-looking blank wall. Dozens of life-forms sat around at cafés and bars, but there was no buzz of conversation. Beings were communicating, but they did not speak. Hands, tentacles, and, occasionally, tongues skittered across the surfaces of small, flat boxes.

Loaf eyed one of the devices more closely. "Those things look like handheld computers." He squared his shoulders. "I'm going to find out what's going on here." He set off toward a building with a large window and a bright awning, which had tables and chairs spilling onto the plaza outside.

Merle put a restraining hand on his sleeve.

"Just don't draw attention to us, okay? We need to keep a low profile."

Loaf scowled. "Forget that. I'm hungry. Let's eat."

The target of Loaf's attentions turned out to be a cyber café. Outside, scores of aliens were tapping messages into their hand-helds. Inside, many more were sending and receiving messages via computer terminals.

Loaf breezed in. The café fell silent as he entered, smiling at all the other customers, who looked at him as though he were crazy. Loaf marched confidently to the serving counter. A six-tentacled, three-eyed, purple being stood behind it. It raised its three eyebrows.

Loaf slapped the counter. "Three Cokes and three pastrami on rye, extra mayo, hold the pickles — oh, and a saucer of milk for the cat."

The being behind the counter jerked back as if Loaf had pulled a gun on it. Glancing around nervously, it hurriedly tapped something out on a keypad at the side of the counter. Strange-looking letters formed on the screen behind its head, almost immediately morphing into familiar, though abbreviated,

English words as the translation program kicked in:

> **Dn't spk 2 me! Use v spokn comunicatn**
> **is prohibitd :-(**

"Hey, no kiddin'!" Loaf turned to the others. "That must be why nobody's talking. Hey, guys, did you see —?"

Jack clamped a hand across Loaf's mouth. He and Merle dragged their struggling companion out of the café.

Loaf squirmed free. "Hey! What's with the rough stuff?"

Merle made frantic shushing motions with her hands. "You'll have the local cops on us. Didn't you read what that guy typed?"

"There's something weird going on here," hissed Jack. "Let's just recharge The Server and teleport out of here."

"We can't risk it," said Merle. "If we hook up The Server, the FOEs may detect it. Until we understand this place, let's just go with the flow. We can still use The Server to communicate."

Loaf looked stubborn. "We still need food."

"How are we going to buy it?" demanded

Merle. "Do you have any alien currency on you?"

Loaf pulled his dad's credit card from his shirt pocket. "We can use this. Good any-where in the Galaxy. Leave this to me." Loaf turned and marched back into the café, with Merle, Jack, and Googie following.

At the counter, Merle tapped on The Server's keyboard and hit the TRANSLATE com-mand. She turned the computer so that the alien could read its screen, which now said, in the language of Deadrock:

Srry abt th mstake. W'd lk sum food.

Loaf waved his dad's credit card invitingly. The shopkeeper examined it suspiciously, sniffed it, nibbled at one edge, then typed the card number into his keypad.

Immediately, the shop was filled with a high-pitched wailing alarm. The shopkeeper ducked behind the counter, and then sprang up, brandishing a slim cylindrical pole. It pointed the device at Loaf and ushered him angrily toward the door.

"I think we're being asked to leave." Goo-

gie was backing away, her ears pressed flat
against her head. "He's got a Bartrakian blowpipe. Those things are illegal in practically
every sector of the Galaxy."

"What do they do?" asked Loaf.

"If you do what he wants, you might get
lucky and never find out. Just shut up and follow me."

Loaf backed out into the plaza and came to
a halt. That was because he had backed into
three walls of muscle. Loaf turned. His gaze
traveled up. And up. And up.

Three aliens stared down emotionlessly at
him. They were dressed in black robes with
white silk scarves around their thick necks.
Their faces were mostly scowls and scar tissue.

One of the nightmarish creatures reached
menacingly inside its robes . . . (Loaf let out a
terrified whimper.) . . . and pulled out a handheld computer. It tapped in a message and
held it out for Loaf to read. It said:

Grtngs. We rpresnt Twista, Grifta,
Sharpie & Bent.

Merle looked quizzically from the aliens to
Loaf and back again. "Friends of yours?"

"Uh . . . hi, guys," stammered Loaf. "Look, if it's about the money for the batteries, they never arrived, so I need to talk to your bosses and work out some amicable . . . urp!" Loaf's voice was cut off as a vicelike hand grabbed him by the neck of his shirt and lifted. Brushing Jack and Merle aside, the gigantic creatures hustled Loaf away.

CHAPTER FIVE

Jack turned to Merle. "We've got to stop them!"

Merle grimaced. "How, exactly? They look as if they eat sharks for breakfast and work out by quarrying granite with their bare hands. How are we going to stop them from tearing Loaf apart?" Her eyes glinted. "After the mess he got us into, do we even want to?"

Jack shot her a horrified glance. "You don't mean that."

Merle sighed. "I guess not. I just don't see what we can do."

"We could go to the authorities. . . ."

Googie hissed. "Not a chance. Haven't you been paying attention? This planet is controlled by the FOEs, and we're number one on

The Tyrant's most wanted list, in case you've forgotten."

Jack clenched his fists in frustration. "There must be *some* way we can help Loaf. . . ."

He broke off suddenly and blinked as someone standing behind him pushed something sharp into the small of his back.

Jack felt his mouth go dry. "Merle," he said, "is somebody holding a knife on me?"

"Well, it's silver and made of metal and it looks sharp and pointy. I don't think it's a hairbrush."

"Fine." Fighting to keep his voice level, Jack asked his unseen adversary, "What do you want me to do?"

A hand appeared over his shoulder and pointed toward a dark alleyway.

"Someday," said Jack as he stepped forward, "maybe we'll end up on a planet where people are pleased to see us. . . ."

Loaf shivered. He had been dragged into a deserted building on the edge of the city by three huge aliens who clearly did not have his best interests at heart. He was sitting on some sort of box, flanked by two muscle-bound hard-beings. Their leader sat facing Loaf, playfully tying a crowbar into knots, and untying it again.

After a moment, it stopped and tapped a message into its handheld computer. Loaf read the screen:

> Lt me state th position clrly. Whn yr crdt
> detls wr fed into th planetary Net, my assocs &
> I wr alertd 2 th fct tht u'v borowd $$$ frm r clnts,
> Twista, Grifta, Sharpie & Bent.
> They wnt thr $$$ back:-(

The alien gave an evil grin and added:

> Wth intrest, v course :-)

"But I never received the goods!" protested Loaf.

The beast shook its head and typed:

> "Thts nt r problm. U shud v
> rd th sml prnt.

"There wasn't any small print!"

> O 'm afrd thr ws. Bt it ws v sml. 2 b spcfc,
> a microdot on th 'i' v Mr. Grifta's nme.
> I admt, it wud b esy 2 miss it unless u

scannd th contract inch by inch with n
electron microscope. Bt I cn assre u,
its cmpltly legally bindng :-)

Sweat poured down Loaf's face. "So how much do I owe?" he asked bitterly.

The alien typed figures into its handheld computer.

U o G$866,000

Loaf turned very pale. In a quavering voice, he asked, "How much is that in U.S. dollars? With interest?"

The alien did the conversion and held out the figures for Loaf to read.

Incldg intrst — Cll it a round 50 billion

Loaf gave a small *urr.*

I hp u'v gt th $$$. Mr. Twista gts vry impatient if he's kpt watng. An't tht rt, boys?

Loaf's interrogator held out the last part of his message to his two hench-things. Each took out a handheld computer and typed in a message which they held out for Loaf to read. The message said:

Hurr-hurr-hurr

The three horrendous beings moved forward, completely surrounding the helpless Loaf.

Jack, Merle, and Googie weren't doing much better.

Their captors ushered them into an alley, where they were blindfolded. They were led into a building and down through what seemed to be a series of tunnels. Eventually, they emerged into the gritty air of the desert, noticeably chilly now. They were bundled into some sort of vehicle, pulled by some being that grunted like a pig and smelled like old bathroom rugs. After a long, bumpy ride, they stopped and were herded through more tunnels before their blindfolds were at last taken off.

They were in a huge sandstone cavern. Fires burned here and there, and flickering lamps hung from the walls or stood on tripods on the uneven floor. Beings of various species sat around the cave, talking, cooking, or cleaning weapons.

Jack blinked and looked around.

The alien who had led them unwrapped a cloth from its mouth. It was humanoid, but with distinctly lizardlike characteristics. Its skin was scaly and tough-looking. Its nostrils were like gill slits, opening and closing when it breathed. Each of its black, expressionless eyes had only one eyelid, which occasionally flickered horizontally across the lens.

The alien spoke. The Server provided an instant translation.

"Welcome, travelers, to our hospitality — however unsought." Their captor made an ironic bow. "And now perhaps you will tell me who you are and what you are doing here?"

Merle stuck out her chin. "Maybe you should tell us who you are and why you kidnapped us, first."

Their captor made a noise that sounded like a chuckle. "The fact that we 'kidnapped' you indicates that we are in a position to ask the questions. Nevertheless — I am J'arl."

Jack looked at him steadily for a moment, then nodded. "All right," he said. "I'm Jack . . . this is Merle, and this is Googie."

J'arl bowed and indicated the laptop, which Merle still carried. "We would particularly like to know how you came to be in possession of this — device." He gave what was unmistakably a smile. "After all, we're all Friends here."

Jack gave a start. "Friends? Do you mean —"

"Shut up!" Googie hissed. "Anyone can call themselves a Friend. It could be a trick."

Their captor turned to the chameleoid and formed two of his flexible fingers into a letter *o* to make the secret sign of the Friends. Googie shrugged noncommittally, and J'arl smiled. "Your caution does you credit. But consider this: You have interpreted our action in bringing you here as 'kidnapping.' Does it not occur to you that we may have saved you from the FOEs? You were wandering around in a strange city, breaking the law with every word you spoke. You would have been arrested by The Tyrant's police within minutes if we had not found you first."

Merle was still unconvinced. "You're talking to us now."

"The Tyrant's rule does not extend here."

"All right. Let's say you rescued us." Merle tilted her head and asked, "Why?"

control

J'arl gave a rueful smile. "I'd like to say out of sheer generosity of spirit. Actually, it had a lot to do with that device you are carrying." Merle clutched The Server protectively.

"All right, let's assume you're telling the truth," said Jack. "But if you're really on our side, why didn't you help us rescue our friend?"

Their captor shook his head. "There was no time. The FOEs police had already been alerted to your presence and any such attempt would have led to your immediate arrest — and ours. The authorities on this world would give a great deal to capture me and the Friends who brought you here. We are the last band of resistance fighters opposing The Tyrant's rule on Deadrock."

Jack was about to speak, but Merle put a hand on his sleeve. "What will happen to Loaf?" she asked.

J'arl lowered his head. "Your friend is in trouble," he said.

Jack nodded. "He owes those thugs money. I don't think they're going to be very polite about asking for it."

"That is the least of his worries," said J'arl

81

grimly. "The creatures who have captured him will soon discover that he is wanted by the FOEs. They are ruthless killers, but they dare not oppose The Tyrant. Your friend will be turned over to the authorities." He fell silent.

Merle prompted, "And then?"

Avoiding her eyes, J'arl said, "And then he will be reformatted."

U.S. Air Force Base, Little Slaughter, near Cambridge, England

Loaf's dad, Master Sergeant Carl Gelt, had just completed a highly profitable (and highly illegal) deal involving surplus equipment (which the air force would have been highly surprised to hear described as "surplus"), when his office was invaded by a powerful-looking man wearing a black suit and dark sunglasses. The master sergeant slammed his phone down hastily and glowered at his visitor. "Didn't anybody ever tell you it's good manners to knock?"

The stranger reached into an inside pocket. "CIA," he said in quiet, cultured tones. He flashed an ID wallet across the sergeant's gaze.

It might have been a CIA badge, but Sergeant Gelt doubted it. He'd used the same trick himself far too often to be fooled. The master sergeant decided to play for time and see what his visitor wanted. After all, he *could* be CIA — or FBI, or any one of a dozen intelligence agencies that Sergeant Gelt knew about — or maybe even one he didn't know about.

The "agent" sat down without invitation and folded his hands in his lap. "I understand you recently came into possession of a laptop computer."

The sergeant had been here before. "I come into possession of a lot of things. It goes with the job. You'll have to refresh my memory."

The agent shook his head sadly. "I do hope you're going to be cooperative, Sergeant."

Master Sergeant Gelt grinned to himself. This guy was no CIA agent. He was a pushover. "Well, I'd like to help you, friend, but I really can't recall. . . ." The master sergeant's smirk froze as a pulse of light flared from his visitor's spectacles, blinding him. Slowly, the sergeant's eyes dulled. His face became expressionless.

The agent reached up and took off his glasses. The illusion-field they had generated melted away. The agent's face blurred and settled into the harsh, gray features of the Bug.

Tracer had picked up Master Sergeant Gelt's name from the financial records of the latest transactions made from The Server and suggested to the Bug that he would be a profitable source of information. The master sergeant had not been difficult to find.

The Bug gazed steadily at Loaf's father. "How did you acquire the computer?"

The master sergeant's voice was low and toneless. "I bought it at a lost property sale. There was some crazy story about a dog carrying it around. It looked like junk, but I had a customer for it."

The alien folded its glasses up and dropped them in its pocket. "What did you do with it?"

"I sold it to Bill Armstrong. One of the construction workers on the base. He wanted it for his boy, Jack. For his birthday."

"Ah." The Bug gave a satisfied nod. "And where is this Jack now?"

"Search me. Loaf might know."

"Who is Loaf?"

"My son, Lothar Gelt."

The Bug was pleased. Jack and Loaf had been the names of the humans captured and interrogated by Tracer before their escape from Kazamblam. A pattern was beginning to form. The Bug continued its questioning.

"Where is Lothar Gelt?"

"He could be anywhere. He doesn't tell me where he's going. Lately, he's been hanging around with the British kid — Jack — and Colonel Stone's daughter."

"Who is Colonel Stone?"

"The big cheese."

"Cheese?" The Bug was puzzled. It shook its wrist-communicator, suspecting a translation glitch. "Are you saying Colonel Stone is formed from curdled milk?"

"No — he's the base commander. His kid's called Merle."

"Fascinating, Sergeant!" The involvement of a girl was new information. Tracer would be very interested when the Bug reported it.

The Bug gave Loaf's father an unpleasant grin. "After I have left, you will remain where you are for a count of one hundred. After that time, you will go about your business. You will

85

have no recollection of my visit or of anything we have discussed. Do you understand?"

Master Sergeant Gelt nodded mechanically. The Bug patted him on the shoulder and walked away. At the door, it turned, took the sunglasses from its pocket, and put them on. Once more it became, to human eyes, a man in a black suit.

"Thank you for your cooperation," it said and left.

A certain scruffy dog, hidden behind a trash can, watched it go.

A'void City, Planet Deadrock, Draco Sector

The three muscle-bound thugs closed in on Loaf, clearly intending to do him serious harm.

"Help!" squeaked Loaf.

A handheld computer beeped urgently. The leader of the thugs held up a hamlike hand, causing his brutal colleagues to halt, and read the incoming message. The horrendous creature began to tremble. It showed the message to its colleagues, who looked terrified.

Then all three sprang into urgent action. With panic-stricken haste, the three bully-beings dragged Loaf out into the dark and deserted streets and hustled him back toward the center of town.

"Where are we going, guys?" Loaf said in a trembling voice.

The chief thug typed a message into his mini-computer and held it for Loaf to read:

Shut up

"Yeah, sure, but hey —" Loaf gibbered, "I can get the money, real soon, you know? Why don't we just sit down and talk about this like reasonable —" He broke off as they stopped before a large building. It had high, solid, windowless walls, topped with barbed wire and dotted with watchtowers, searchlights, and gun emplacements.

Loaf said, "Um . . . this isn't a hotel. Am I right?"

The chief hench-being tapped out another message.

Ths is th FOEs HQ on Deadrock. U r chckng in. Th Tyrant wnts u :-(

A shove in the back propelled Loaf through a huge steel door that slammed behind him with a very final sound.

A beam of light shot from somewhere high above Loaf. He stood rooted to the spot, unable to move. Words began to form on a screen in front of him.

WELCOME.

"Yeah, er, hi . . ." stuttered Loaf, peering apprehensively into the darkness.

DO NOT BE ALARMED.

"Right. Okay."

BE ABSOLUTELY PETRIFIED, LOTHAR GELT.

Loaf was on the verge of tears. "What are you going to do to me?"

YOUR MIND WILL BE PROBED, WASHED, AND
HUNG OUT TO DRY. THEN YOU WILL BE REFORMATTED.
DO NOT BE CONCERNED.

The words continued to flow, ignoring Loaf's screams and pleas for mercy.

→ **control**

THE REFORMATTING PROCESS IS
COMPARATIVELY PAINLESS.

"Compared to what?" shrieked Loaf.

OH, TO BEING ROASTED TO DEATH OVER A SLOW
FIRE, SAY, OR EATEN ALIVE BY ANTS. BUT
CONSIDER THE BENEFITS.

Loaf gibbered with terror as the letters on
the screen inexorably spelled out his doom.

SOON, YOU WILL BE ONE OF US.

CHAPTER SIX

Roadside Diner, Little Slaughter, near Cambridge, England

The sky was darkening as an oddly shaped figure crept out of the woods and cautiously made its way toward the Flying Griddle Snack Bar and Roadside Diner. It broke cover, pelted across the deserted parking lot, and disappeared around the back. Moments later, a keen-eared listener would have caught the sound of something rummaging through trash cans.

The portly alien life-form, having dived straight into a Dumpster, was now upside down with its legs waving in the air. After a lot of wriggling and grunting, it managed to extricate itself. It stood up, brushing some stray lettuce leaves from the Arcadia Theme Park uniform it had been wearing when Bitz had accidentally teleported it to Earth along with

Jack, Loaf, and Merle. For a moment, it crouched, its two heads weaving suspiciously, making sure that it had not attracted attention. Then it regarded its prize.

"Bwarp!" it said with satisfaction.

It was holding a Styrofoam burger box. Slobbering with anticipation, it opened the container to reveal an almost perfect double cheeseburger. Only one bite had been taken from it — by a customer in a hurry, perhaps, or one who had recognized the taste of gristle laced with monosodium glutamate. The ALF licked its lips with its long, purple tongue. Then it threw away the burger and ate the styrofoam box, crunching up the pieces in sheer bliss.

It finished the last piece of packaging and burped appreciatively.

"Well now, what have we here?"

The ALF's six eyes nearly popped with terror. It spun around and flattened itself against the wooden wall of the snack bar. Since it had escaped from the air force base, it had been living rough in the woods. And for an alien life-form whose digestive system wasn't designed to cope with anything that Earth-creatures considered food, that meant *rough*. It had been watching this place for days — there shouldn't have been any humans out at this time.

There weren't.

The Bug stepped out from the shadows. The ALF gulped. Its legs began to shake. The ALF wasn't too bright, but it knew all about Bugs. Every advanced species in the Galaxy knew that the most sensible thing to do if a Bug was looking for you was to change your name, move to another planet, and jump off a very high cliff.

The Bug advanced on the ALF, which closed its eyes and whimpered. Bitz, crouching behind a garbage bag, held his breath. Surely the Bug wasn't going to —?

The Bug loomed over the ALF. "Do you want to get off this planet?"

The ALF opened its eyes again. Hope dawned in them. "Bwarp?"

The Bug beckoned to it. "I have a little job for you. . . ."

Freedom Fighters Headquarters, Planet Deadrock, Draco Sector

J'arl had refused to answer any more questions from Jack and Merle until they had eaten. Despite their concern about Loaf's predicament, they ate ravenously. Googie had turned her nose up at the offered meal.

"This is worse than that foul canned stuff you made me eat," she complained bitterly to Merle.

Merle gave her pet an offended look. "You always had the best food in the store."

"Oh, wonderful. Textured vegetable protein, mixed with who-knows-what and preserved in jelly — *jelly,* for crying out loud." Googie shook her head and sneezed. "Yum-yum. Thank you *sooo* much."

Jack gulped down a mouthful. "How are we going to rescue Loaf?"

J'arl shook his head. "He may already be past help. I cannot ask my people to risk their lives for the sake of a stranger who may already have become a spy for the enemy. . . ."

"But Loaf's our friend," protested Jack.

93

J'arl gave him a knowing look. "Yes, but is your friend a Friend?"

Jack stared. "What?"

"Wellll . . ." said Merle doubtfully. "It is his fault we're all in this mess."

Jack caught on. "Of course Loaf's a Friend," he said hurriedly. "He helped us rescue The Server." Merle raised her eyebrows at this piece of historical inaccuracy. "Friends should stick together through thick and thin. You don't just give up on a Friend because he makes one mistake. We can't abandon him."

J'arl considered. "But what would we gain from a rescue attempt? We are safe here, but if we attempted a raid on the city . . ."

"Where exactly is 'here'?" asked Merle.

"We are in a desert area some distance from A'void. It is a place known as Dead Beings' Gulch."

Jack remembered the long stretch of country they had crossed to reach the cave. "Good name."

J'arl explained that Dead Beings' Gulch was an area of canyons, chasms, caverns, and other deep holes beginning with *c*. For this reason, it was a perfect hiding place for a group of rebel fighters.

"But this is your planet, isn't it?" asked Jack. "Why are you in hiding?"

"I am no storyteller." J'arl beckoned another member of his own species forward. The figure was smaller than J'arl and its movements were more graceful. Female? Jack wondered.

"C'aran has made a study of Deadrock's past," said J'arl. "She can tell you our unhappy history better than I."

With The Server translating, C'aran told the story of how Deadrock had once been a vibrant trading world. Many Friends had lived on Deadrock and an Outernet Server had been established on the planet.

At the mention of this Server, there was a murmur of discontent from the other fighters. Merle shot Jack a quizzical glance, which he returned with a shrug.

C'aran continued with the tale of how Deadrock had been invaded by the FOEs and of the desperate resistance put up by the Friends. A valiant attempt to counter the invasion had proved futile. Most of those who had fought for freedom were soon overwhelmed by FOEs forces and defeated. Deadrock had become yet another conquered planet.

As the cavern fires burned low, C'aran came to the end of the story. "Those Friends who survived fled to the desert and took refuge in these underground caverns. We try to defy The Tyrant, but out here it is hard enough merely to survive."

She fell silent. J'arl nodded his thanks.

Jack was puzzled. "But how does The Tyrant keep control? We didn't see any soldiers or police in A'void."

J'arl gave a bitter laugh. "You would have, had we not found you first. But the FOEs don't need soldiers on the streets. One of The Tyrant's first actions was to take over the Deadrock Server and twist it to serve his ends. His next move was to ban all forms of verbal communication on pain of death. No being is allowed to talk with another — all forms of communication have to be electronic and are routed through The Tyrant's Server."

"I don't understand," said Jack. "Why did he do that?"

"Surely that's obvious," drawled Googie in a superior voice. "It means that everything can be monitored. Every message, every conversation, every transaction. The FOEs know everything that happens on this planet."

J'arl nodded gravely. "You tell me that Deadrock has a bad reputation because no one who comes here ever leaves. Now you know why. It is forbidden. Outgoing t-mail is forbidden. Departing ships carry only The Tyrant's forces. No one else can leave."

"But why do your people put up with it?" demanded Merle. "Why don't you rebel?"

"It is impossible for the people of Deadrock to revolt against The Tyrant." J'arl's voice was quiet, but angry. "No one can reveal their true feelings to another without simultaneously revealing them to the FOEs. We can have thoughts and dreams of rebellion and revolt, but we cannot communicate them. If any being has anything to say against The Tyrant or the system on Deadrock, the FOEs know about it instantly."

"Isolate and rule," nodded Googie. "A classic FOE tactic for subjugating conquered species." The chameleoid thought it better not to mention that, as a former agent of The Tyrant, it was a tactic she had often used.

"What happens if anyone does say something against the FOEs?" asked Merle.

"Such beings are picked up and taken away," said J'arl. "The lucky ones are reformatted."

Jack's thoughts returned to Loaf. "What does that mean?"

"The FOEs use computers controlled by the Deadrock Server to reprogram the mind. Any being that is reformatted becomes a creature of The Tyrant."

Merle gave a whistle. "That's a seriously heavy control mechanism."

Jack looked horrified. "So that's what could happen on our home planet if The Tyrant got ahold of our Server?"

J'arl nodded. "Yet your Server could be of use to us." He looked from Jack to Merle and back again. "The only hope of freedom for us is to destroy the corrupted Server that controls our lives on this planet. Every communication and surveillance device on this planet is routed through and controlled by the Deadrock server. We know that it is kept in what used to be the home of the government on our planet: the Krumblin."

Merle raised an eyebrow. "The Krumblin?"

"Yes, it's a very old building — the building, in fact, opposite the café where I picked you up. We have plans to attack it. But the FOEs server is kept in a sealed vault, behind an impregnable door surrounded by powerful force fields. We could never hope to breach it.

"But with the proper access codes, we could get into the vault. We could destroy the Deadrock server. To do that, we need another machine of equal power." He indicated The Server. "You possess one."

Jack nodded.

"So here is my proposition." J'arl looked hard at Jack. "By now, your friend will be a prisoner in the FOEs headquarters. We will rescue the human — providing you then come with us to the Krumblin. We will use your Server to give us access to the device that controls our lives, so that we may destroy it."

U.S. Air Force Base, Little Slaughter,
near Cambridge, England

"Sorry to disturb you, Colonel. Two gentle-men wish to see you." An orderly stood apolo-getically at Colonel Stone's door.

Merle's father looked tired. His eyes were bloodshot. "I thought I said I wasn't to be dis-turbed."

"Yes, sir. Sorry, sir. That's what I told them." The orderly's voice was slow and deliberate, almost robotic. "They were very insistent."

"Indeed we were." The orderly was pushed aside by a huge, black-suited figure. A smaller figure sidled into the room in its wake.

The colonel glared at them. "This had bet-ter be important. . . ." He was interrupted by a clamor of barking from outside and turned to stare out the window. A dog was leaping at the glass, scratching at it with its claws, and yap-ping furiously.

Colonel Stone shot a furious glance at his orderly. "Airman — there's a crazy dog trying to get in here. Do you think *that's* something you can deal with?"

The unhappy orderly saluted. "Yes, sir.

Sorry, sir. Right away, sir." He went out. Moments later, the insistent yapping was cut off by a roar of rage. The sounds of pursuit faded into the distance.

The first intruder smiled complacently and raised a hand cupped around a wallet. It was opened to reveal an ID card. "Agent Bugatti, CIA. When did you last see your daughter, Colonel?"

Colonel Stone sat down abruptly. He'd been wondering that very same thing. The last time he'd actually *seen* Merle had been before he went out on Saturday night. He'd not looked in on her on his return because he'd arrived home very late from his office. He'd glanced into her room on Sunday morning, and she'd apparently been in bed, though he hadn't looked too closely. An urgent phone call had summoned him to a meeting in London. He hadn't returned until late. This morning, he'd discovered a fake "body" in Merle's bed. There was no telling how long she'd been gone.

To make matters worse, two of Merle's friends were also missing. Their families were calling him on an hourly basis. Major Jackson's men were making discreet inquiries on the base, and Colonel Stone was considering calling in the British police.

Agent Bugatti was guaranteed Colonel Stone's full attention. The Bug, secure in its disguise, knew this very well. What it had learned from Master Sergeant Gelt, coupled with Tracer's background information, was proving very valuable in breaking through the Earthman's defenses.

After all, it was all in The Tyrant's basic training manual. Go straight to the top. Control the head being, and you control the whole organization. *In this case,* the Bug thought smugly, *get to the girl through the father, but get to the father through the relationship with his daughter.*

The Bug had been less sure about Tracer's suggestion to recruit the ALF to help deal with the Friends agent Sirius. The chameleoid was known to still be on Earth and would have to be watched. The Bug would need to concentrate on the task of controlling Colonel Stone. This would leave the ALF to keep all six eyes peeled for Sirius, who seemed to have taken the form of a dog — probably the one that had been barking at the window a moment ago. The Bug smiled to itself. One thing at a time.

"Sit down, Colonel," the Bug said, casting a warning glance at the ALF, which was about to compromise its disguise by eating a small plastic American flag from the colonel's desk. The ALF hurriedly put the flag down. "I'm sorry to say that your daughter has become involved in a covert operation. I need to speak to her immediately."

The colonel was not used to receiving orders from strangers. His suspicious nature kicked in. "I need to check your credentials, Agent Bugatti." He reached toward his phone.

The Bug placed its hand on the receiver.

"That won't be necessary, Colonel," it said smoothly. "Don't you agree?"

The Bug touched a concealed switch on the side of its dark glasses. A burst of light pulsed from the lenses. The colonel's outraged face immediately smoothed into a mask of passivity.

Having evaded the orderly's search, Bitz returned to Colonel Stone's window just in time to see the colonel fall completely under the Bug's control. The Friends agent continued his desperate attempts to attract attention, but in his heart, he knew that he was already too late.

CHAPTER SEVEN

Planet Deadrock, Draco Sector

The creatures that pulled the freedom fighters' carts looked even worse than they smelled.

Jack asked J'arl what they were called, and
the response had been a noise like someone
spitting in a bucket. The Server had been unable to provide a translation. For several
hours, the small army of desert raiders had
marched through the freezing night, moving
along hidden trails between brooding sandstone cliffs. Jack had spent most of the time
huddled under animal skins, desperately trying to keep warm, and staring at the huge,
purple, hairy bottoms of the animals pulling
the cart — whatever they were called.

Jack had been surprised and alarmed to
see that the band of raiders was very lightly

armed for an attack on a heavily defended target. Most of the freedom fighters had swords and daggers, and some had blowpipes or bows and arrows. A few carried packs filled with what looked like primitive bombs, but none carried any kind of gun. The few vehicles in the caravan had no engines. Instead, they were pulled by pack animals. Jack wondered whether this was due simply to lack of equipment — or to choice. The Friends on Deadrock seemed to have little enthusiasm for machines of any kind.

At the edge of A'void City, screened by dunes, the raiders had uncovered a series of unused wells, dropping down into tunnels that ran under the desert and beneath a large part of the city. J'arl had told Jack during their march through these passages that the tunnels had once been watercourses. Deadrock's rivers had retreated underground long ago and carved these channels in the soft rock. But now even the underground streams had sunk deep within the planet and could only be reached by boreholes. The tunnels had been left to the creepy-crawly things normally found in such places — and to those whose opposition to The Tyrant made their appearance above ground dangerous in the extreme.

Eventually, J'arl called a halt.

Speaking very softly, he said, "We are now very close to the FOEs headquarters. Rest now. Try and get some sleep. We will attack just before first light. Do not worry. We will save your friend."

Merle was cold, tired, and grouchy. "Great," she muttered wearily. "Hip-hip who cares?"

U.S. Air Force Base, Little Slaughter, near Cambridge, England

Major Hal Jackson first knew of the arrival of two CIA operatives when he walked into Colonel Stone's office and met them.

Major Jackson didn't like CIA involvement in military affairs. He didn't like the CIA, period. One of the CIA men who currently occupied the base commander's office was tall and heavily built and looked like a thug, though he spoke like a college professor. The other was short and tubby and looked nervous.

"Hal," Colonel Stone was saying, "I want you to offer Agent Bugatti and Agent Alford every possible assistance."

Jackson shifted uncomfortably. "Yes, sir."

Major Jackson was ill at ease. As head of base security, he should have been informed of the CIA men's arrival. Supposing they *were* CIA men — but that was ridiculous. Frank Stone was no fool. He must have checked their credentials, surely? As the colonel's aide, Jackson could hardly ask his commanding officer whether he'd followed basic security procedures. The major felt he was losing his grip on events. What was more, there was a dog bouncing up and down outside the colonel's office window yapping furiously, and the noise was giving him a headache.

Also, there was something about the CIA men that bothered Jackson. In spite of their reputation, CIA agents didn't really wear dark glasses *all* the time. The one who called himself Agent Bugatti treated Frank Stone as if the colonel was a flunky; and Stone, who had been known to outface five-star generals, made no protest. Also, Agent Alford hadn't spoken a word throughout the whole meeting.

Agent Bugatti was speaking. "I have informed Colonel Stone," he said calmly, "that his daughter, Merle, has inadvertently come into possession of a . . . device, which resembles an ordinary laptop computer. In reality, this device is a strictly classified and highly dangerous piece of equipment belonging to the U.S. government. We want it back."

The CIA man paused. Major Jackson gave him a thin smile. That might explain Agent Alford — he was probably some computer geek brought in as a civilian advisor. Trust the CIA to develop something they didn't understand, and then lose it. Jackson turned to the shorter CIA man. "Specifically, what sort of device are we discussing?"

Agent Alford looked at the carpet and muttered something Jackson didn't quite catch. It sounded like "Bwarp."

"The nature of the device is classified," Agent Bugatti interrupted smoothly. Jackson shot him an angry glance.

"Merle Stone," Agent Bugatti continued, "has no idea of the device's true nature or of how dangerous it could be. Her current whereabouts are unknown. But if she — or her known associates, Jack Armstrong or Lothar Gelt — appears on this base, she must be apprehended using all necessary force."

Major Jackson's jaw dropped. He turned to his chief. "Colonel?"

"You heard the man, Major!" Stone's voice was harsh. "This base is on full alert as of now. If any of your men find my daughter or her friends, they are to be arrested on sight and Agents Bugatti and Alford are to be informed immediately."

Jackson shot a look at Agent Bugatti and longed to wipe the complacent smile off his face, but he only said, "Yes, sir."

A'void City, Planet Deadrock, Draco Sector

Jack's mouth was dry as he crouched in the red-walled tunnel, awaiting the order to attack. Merle sat against the opposite tunnel wall, hunched over The Server, her expression tight-lipped. Googie was washing herself with assumed nonchalance, but her fur bristled with tension nevertheless.

Jack turned to J'arl, who was waiting just ahead of him. "Don't think I'm complaining, but your people only have swords and bows and arrows and stuff. How can you hope to win against guards armed with Slay-o-matic energy pistols and Maxi-wound laser cannons?"

J'arl gave him a wicked grin. "Like this."

He signaled to the commando unit behind them. Jack and Merle were left behind as the squad suddenly surged through the tunnel, up a ladder set in a vertical shaft, and out into the open ground that lay before the FOEs headquarters.

The speed and silence of the raiders from the desert were breathtaking. Some of the fighters raised their blowpipes to send tranquilizer darts buzzing like hornets toward the lookouts on the guard towers, who instantly collapsed. Others, weaving between searchlight beams, reached the foot of the high walls and swung grappling hooks over the parapets. More fighters swarmed arm over arm up the ropes like ants climbing a tree trunk.

The FOEs were caught completely unaware by the suddenness of the attack. One minute, the night shift was yawning through an uneventful watch and looking forward to being relieved at dawn. The next, they were being set upon by swarms of red-robed attackers, their warning cries instantly muffled.

At last, the defenders woke up to the fact that their headquarters had been invaded, and someone more alert than the rest sounded the alarm. Immediately, the silent attackers set up a cacophony of screams, yells, and roars, mixed with the clash of swords and explosions of homemade smoke grenades. The defenders who managed to get to their guns found themselves firing at shadows in the dense smoke that suddenly filled every room and corridor. The desert raiders, accustomed to fighting in low light and poor visibility, harried their panic-stricken enemies, who broke and ran. The retreat quickly became chaotic.

By the time Jack (carrying Googie) and Merle (carrying The Server) had found their way into the FOEs prison, the fighting was all but over. Sporadic flashes from the windows showed that the freedom fighters continued to pursue their fleeing enemies out into the city, but the Headquarters building was under rebel control.

J'arl emerged from the smoke and took Jack's arm. "Come. We have little time. They

will soon regroup. When reinforcements ar-
rive they will overwhelm us if we remain."

C'aran ran in to report. "We have located
the human prisoner in the detention block.
This way."

Guided by the rebels, Jack and Merle stum-
bled down smoke-filled corridors. With her superior night vision, Googie skipped over the
debris of the fight, but Jack and Merle skinned
knees and knuckles in falls. They reached the
cells just as two freedom fighters dragged a
coughing Loaf out of his cell.

Jack grabbed him by the arms. "Are you
okay?"

Loaf coughed again. "I *was*. What *is* this
stuff? Who are these guys?"

"We'll play Twenty Questions later." If
Merle was relieved at Loaf's rescue, she was
hiding it extremely well. "What did they do to
you?"

"Well, they asked me all kinds of questions. . . ."

"Did they reformat you?"

Loaf looked panic-stricken for a moment,
then he shook his head and said, "That was on
the schedule for tomorrow."

"You sure about that?" Merle eyed Loaf narrowly. "You sure you haven't been turned into a mindless slave of The Tyrant?" Loaf stared at her, speechless. Merle turned to J'arl. "How can you tell if someone's been re-formatted?"

"They become treacherous, weak, cowardly, pitiable creatures, frightened of their own shadows and caring only for self-preservation."

Googie gave Loaf a hard stare. "No difference there, then."

Loaf bridled. "Hey!"

"I guess we'll just have to take his word for it," said Merle.

"We must make our escape immediately." J'arl's urgent voice cut off the exchange. "The FOEs will summon reinforcements and attack us at any moment. I am surprised that they have not done so already. . . ."

J'arl broke off as an aide ran in and made his report in a series of barking grunts. J'arl listened intently, then turned back to Jack and Merle, his face grim.

"Reinforcements have indeed arrived from the T'em'ul barracks, but they are not being sent to attack us. They have formed an armed barrier around the entire city. I am afraid, my Friends, that the FOEs have outmaneuvered us. They used your friend as bait, and I have led us straight into a trap."

Merle gave a gasp, and Loaf whimpered. Jack said, "What can we do?"

J'arl gave a grim smile. "Disappear. It's something we're good at, and we have Friends in the city. But first, we will make sure that the FOEs remember this visit."

J'arl signaled, and the raiding party set explosives (borrowing them from the FOEs arsenal when their own ran out). Then they made a hasty retreat. A few minutes later, a titanic explosion rocked the city. By the time the FOEs reinforcements arrived, their headquarters was a smoking ruin, and there was no sign at all of the desert raiders.

In his temporary hideout in the cellar beneath a furniture warehouse, J'arl and his lieutenants held a council of war with Jack, Merle, Loaf, and Googie.

J'arl's voice was weary. "We have won a battle," he said, "but in doing so, we have lost the war. The mission to rescue your fellow human has cost us dearly. The FOEs are now on their guard, and any attempt to storm the Krumblin and destroy the Deadrock server would be futile. What is more, this is the end of the resistance to the FOEs on Deadrock. We cannot remain hidden long in the city. The FOEs have spies and informers everywhere. We will be tracked down and killed, one by one."

Jack said nothing. There seemed to be nothing to say.

"Therefore," J'arl continued, "your Server is of no further use to us, but it will be used against us when it falls, as it most surely will, into the hands of our enemies."

Merle eyed him apprehensively. "What are you saying?"

"That device you carry cannot help my people. It will be used to harm us. Give it to me." J'arl's voice was relentless. "It must be destroyed."

CHAPTER EIGHT

Jack picked up The Server and pulled it to his chest protectively. "What good is destroying this going to do?" he protested.

J'arl pointed at The Server. "This technology has brought destruction to our planet. We do not need such technology. We should look to our past."

"You're wrong!" insisted Merle. "You can't live in the past. Things move on. That's how civilization works. If it didn't, everyone would still be living in caves."

"We are," J'arl pointed out.

Merle groaned. "Maybe I could have put that better. . . ."

"Merle's right," said Jack. "You're behaving like ostriches."

There was a puzzled silence as the freedom fighters looked at one another blankly.

"Ostriches are huge birds on our planet," explained Jack. "They live in desert areas, and at the first sign of danger, they stick their heads in the sand. They try to ignore what's going on."

"We do not ignore danger," J'arl bristled. "You have experience of that fact."

Jack shook his head. "That's not what I mean." He struggled for another example. "It's like, when I'm in bed at night and hear a strange noise, I put my pillow over my head and pretend it's not there or, if it is, it'll go away."

"Jack's right," Merle said. "You can't live in the past. Technology won't go away. You can't destroy knowledge once it's out there. It's like toothpaste."

"Toothpaste?"

"You can't put toothpaste back in the tube," said Jack.

"You can't put the genie back in the bottle," added Merle.

"You can't put the legs back on the spider," said Loaf.

Merle and Jack turned and gave him disgusted looks.

Loaf looked puzzled. "What?"

J'arl was clearly baffled. "I'm afraid you've lost me."

"The point is," said Merle, "once something's invented, it stays invented. You can't deny or ignore it. You can't turn back the clock."

J'arl considered. "But this technology is causing us harm. Therefore, it must be destroyed." He moved toward Jack.

Jack held The Server tightly.

"It's not technology that's bad, it's the way you use it." Everyone turned toward Googie.

"Technology is neither good nor bad," continued the chameleoid.

"Googie's right," exclaimed Jack. "The Weaver set up the Outernet so that all races in the Galaxy could exchange information and ideas. It was meant to promote understanding and progress. The servers were supposed to help people."

J'arl shook his head. "But it is through the Deadrock server that The Tyrant controls us. And the FOEs will be waiting for us if we attempt to raid the Krumblin."

"You guys are stuck in the past," said Merle. "And if you live in the past, you think in the past. Your enemies are living in the electronic age! You don't have to break down castle walls to get at them. You don't even need to force your way in. There are other ways." Merle paused for effect. "We can use technology to beat technology."

"And how is this to be achieved?" responded J'arl.

Merle looked J'arl straight in the eye. "I have an idea," she said. "Trust me."

J'arl considered for a few seconds before nodding. "I will speak with the others and put it to a vote." He and the other raiders went into a tense huddle.

Jack turned to Merle. "What's the idea?" he whispered.

"I'll tell you after they've made up their minds."

"It had better be good," whined Loaf. "If they don't like it, they'll destroy The Server and we won't be able to get home."

Googie gave a worried meow. "I don't want to spend the rest of my life here. Being stuck on Earth was bad enough. . . ."

They sank into silence as J'arl continued to talk with the fighters. There were growls and raised voices before the discussion ended.

J'arl walked back over, looking grave. "We have considered your argument," he said. "We will listen to your plan."

Loaf gave a whoop and was instantly shushed. Jack and Merle breathed sighs of relief.

"But," continued J'arl, "if you fail, we will destroy The Server."

If I fail, thought Merle, *you won't have to —* *the FOEs will have done it for you.*

U.S. Air Force Base, Little Slaughter, near Cambridge, England

The dog was back.

The Bug smiled. The heightened threat condition of the past couple of days had forced the Friends agent to go into hiding, but as the first tense hours of the alert had relaxed into something more normal, the chameleoid had returned.

As Janus's partner, Bitz was accustomed to

following the senior agent's plans. At the moment, he was at a loss. Not being able to talk, he couldn't tell Colonel Stone about the Bug. Maybe he could attract the colonel's attention by biting him in the rear, or he could try to wreck the Bug's wrist communicator. Bitz was desperate and short of ideas. But he had to keep trying.

The Tyrant's enforcer turned to Colonel Stone. "Colonel," it said, "I'd like you to go and look out the window."

The Colonel stood up. Merle's father, after two days of the Bug's mind control, didn't look well. His face had an unhealthy pallor. He was sweating. He was clearly fighting against the Bug's invasion of his mind. The Bug frowned. If the girl didn't make contact soon with her father, it would have to take decisive action.

Colonel Stone stared out the window. Bitz went completely berserk in his attempts to warn the base commander, jumping up, clawing at the glass, and yapping his head off, oblivious to everything else. Behind the colonel's back, the Bug looked meaningfully at its smaller colleague and gave a prearranged signal. The ALF looked unhappy but obediently sidled out of the room.

Outside the window, the dog was too busy jumping and yapping at Colonel Stone to notice that he was being stalked. The ALF made a sudden grab for the dog and disappeared from view. There was a muffled yelp, then a furious growling and a scream of pain that sounded like audio feedback. The ALF staggered into view. Its dark glasses slipped. For a moment, Colonel Stone saw a small two-headed figure. The dog had its teeth clamped on the nose of one of the heads, and its victim was flailing its arms to try to dislodge it. The colonel closed his eyes. His hands began to tremble.

The Bug reached past the colonel's shoulder and swiftly lowered the blind, picking up the conversation as though nothing had happened. "All this unpleasantness will be over once we have made contact with your daughter, Colonel," it said soothingly. "But you must understand that, under the circumstances, the girl must be detained for her own protection."

Just for a moment, Colonel Stone's face twisted as if he was engaged in some internal struggle. Then he sat down and looked up. "Her own protection," he said tonelessly.

The Bug allowed itself a satisfied smile. It was fortunate that the habits of obedience were deeply ingrained in these Earth-humans. The Bug's grin broadened. The Tyrant would love them!

The office door crashed open. Bitz, closely pursued by the panting ALF, flew in. The chameleoid launched himself at the Bug in a desperate and futile attack.

With an agility that belied its size, the FOEs agent managed to sidestep Bitz's frenzied charge. "Shut the door," it commanded, brushing off yet another assault.

The ALF obeyed, then glanced toward the desk, worrying about the Earth-man's reaction to this sudden turn of events. It needn't have bothered. The colonel merely sat in his chair like a lifeless shell.

Bitz stood panting and growling as he prepared himself for a further attack.

"Come on, Friend," whispered the Bug menacingly. From the depths of its suit, it took a brightly colored piece of plastic and formed it into a noose.

Bitz glanced toward the communication device on the Bug's forearm. If he could destroy that, he'd stop the Bug from being able to contact its superiors. Then the Bug would be relatively harmless.

Bitz leaped again, aiming for his enemy's wrist. As he did so, he felt himself being lassoed. He froze in midair and dropped to the floor. There was a collar around his neck!

"Oowwwlllllll!" A burning sensation coursed through Bitz's body. He struggled for breath as the choke collar closed around his neck, cutting off his windpipe. His tongue lolled out as he tried to breathe — it was impossible. His life was being choked out of him. He felt his eyes begin to bulge and he sank to the ground.

Suddenly, he could breathe again. He panted in air, lungful after lungful, and stood up ready to renew his attack on the FOE.

"Owwwlll!" Again the burning sensation, again he was unable to breathe.

The Bug stood over Bitz, smiling. Its gray hand was hovering over the communications device that was also controlling the choke collar. "I have total control over you," it purred. "Shall I continue?"

Bitz could only stare up at the huge figure.

"Or I could crush you." The Bug lifted its tree trunk of a leg above the stricken chameleoid.

Bitz closed his eyes. I've failed, he thought, and waited for the end.

It didn't come. He found he could suddenly breathe again. He lay wheezing and panting on the ground, unable to get up.

The Bug laughed. "No. I need you, so I do hope you are going to behave." It patted the control device. "You're going to help me get The Server. . . ."

A'void City, Planet Deadrock, Draco Sector

Jack, Merle, and Loaf were sitting with C'aran in front of a computer terminal at the cyber café in the A'void City plaza, beneath the decaying walls of the Krumblin. A variety of lifeforms sat (or floated) around them, drinking, eating, and communicating via their handheld computers.

J'arl stood at the counter, ordering food and

drinks. He was in disguise, dressed in the robes of a Valudian door-to-door sales-thing. It was a perfect disguise — no being with any sense would ever wish to communicate with a Valudian door-to-door sales-thing. As he moved through the café, he nodded discreetly to other diners and to a number of figures spread throughout the plaza, leaning against buildings, lounging on benches. At least some of J'arl's desert raiders had responded to his summons.

Several hours earlier, J'arl had agreed to Merle's plan. After resting, he and C'aran dispatched their lieutenants to bring as many of the raiders as they could find to the plaza beneath the Krumblin walls. Then J'arl had led the humans carefully through A'void. They were dressed in long, flowing desert robes that had been smuggled into their hideout by C'aran. These costumes had the benefit of disguising their features and protecting them from the high temperatures and stinging sand as they sneaked, carefully dodging FOE patrols, through the silent streets of the city.

Jack had been reluctant to include Loaf in this expedition. He had discussed the problem with J'arl.

"Has he been reformatted? Has he become a spy for the FOEs?" Jack shrugged unhappily. "I can't tell. I need time to watch him. If he comes with us, I can't be sure he won't betray us."

"It is a risk," agreed J'arl, "but we have no choice. We cannot leave him here, I cannot spare the guards. The rest of my band are scattered. I cannot contact them. Only a few of us remain to carry out the attack. We will watch him closely. At the first sign of treachery . . ."

J'arl had left the sentence unfinished, but his meaning was clear enough. If Loaf had been reformatted, he would be . . . shut down.

Merle took off the backpack she was carrying, set it on her knee, and opened it. A whiskered face peered out, breathing hard. Googie leaped onto the table, directed a filthy look at Merle, and started to wash herself in a very pointed manner.

J'arl returned to the terminal with glasses of a black-and-green liquid and a plate of food. Jack and Merle stared wide-eyed at the small, multilimbed creatures spread out on the plate. Some of them were still moving.

Unable to speak, Merle and Jack shook

their heads and gave a mental *uuurggghh!* Googie licked her lips. Loaf gawked at the plate in horror.

Other beings in the café began to stare at the group. J'arl gestured urgently to the humans that they should drink and eat. C'aran popped something wriggly into her mouth and gave Jack an encouraging smile. Jack decided to brave it. He picked up one of the creatures, popped it into his mouth, and bit down. His face turned a pale shade of green as he chewed on the local delicacy.

The customers in the café returned to their own business.

As Jack continued to crunch on his "dinner," C'aran offered Loaf a tidbit that seemed to be all eyes and legs. Loaf looked up to see the nightmarish snack hovering in front of his face. He swatted at the offering, which dropped down the front of his robes.

With a hoarse cry of alarm, Loaf thrust his hands beneath his robes and scrambled desperately for the alien morsel. "Gedditoff!" he shrieked. "It's biting me!"

Merle and Jack tried desperately to shush

him. J'arl clasped his hand over Loaf's mouth, but it was too late. The café patrons were staring at the group in horror. The proprietor recognized Loaf and whipped out its handheld computer.

U again!

The café proprietor went for its blowpipe. Instantly, it felt a razor-sharp knife prickling its skin in the vicinity of some major organs whose sudden loss would be seriously inconvenient.

"Touch any alarms," hissed the voice of C'aran in what passed for the creature's ear, "and you are a dead-being."

She pried the blowpipe from the unhappy alien's tentacles. The café customers saw the throwing knife in C'aran's hand and sensibly decided that all this disturbance had nothing to do with them. By the time a FOEs patrol appeared in the plaza, staring around suspiciously and fingering their weapons, the other customers had resumed their virtual conversations.

J'arl and C'aran faked attitudes of casual relaxation. The proprietor made a great show of polishing their table, nervously aware of

C'aran's concealed knife, which was still poised to do irreparable harm. Jack and Merle sat in rigid terror, chewing uncomfortably.

As soon as the patrol had left the square, Jack grabbed Loaf by the shoulder and put his lips right next to his ear. "You did that on purpose!" he hissed angrily.

Loaf shook him off. "She dropped that thing inside my shirt! I couldn't help it. It wriggled!"

"Shut up!" Jack looked Loaf straight in the eye. Had he been reformatted? Or was he just being Loaf? "One more false move," he whispered, "and you're cat-meat."

"No, thanks." Googie wrinkled her nose.

"Oh, c'mon, Jack." Loaf laughed nervously. "You know me."

"Yes, I do. If you take one more step out of line, I'll turn you over to C'aran. I'm watching you. Think about it."

As Loaf shifted sweatily in his chair, J'arl slid into the seat next to Merle. "You must act quickly," he murmured. "Some of the beings in this café may be FOEs. Messages may already be on the way to The Tyrant. Contact the Deadrock server. Do it now!"

Merle nodded, removed The Server's carrying case from her shoulder, and pulled the computer out. She opened the case and followed J'arl's instructions to connect to the Deadrock server.

"Last night," she explained, "I set up The Server's translator as a decryption program. It'll run every possible combination of numbers in the Deadrock server's access codes until they match up. Then we can instruct it to let us in." She crossed her fingers. "Here goes."

Merle initiated the program and watched the screen, nodding in satisfaction as the number sequences matched up. Here and there, figures stopped flickering and glowed red as The Server identified a digit of the Deadrock access code. At this rate, they'd have access to the Krumblin in a few seconds.

Suddenly, Merle's look turned to a frown. Numbers that had been red had returned to white and started flickering again. "That shouldn't be happening. I need Help."

There was no response from the cranky hologram. Merle rapped its casing. "Hey, Help! Come on out here!"

Help failed to appear. A dialogue box appeared in one corner of the screen.

ArE we oFf DeaDRocK YeT?

Merle clenched her fists. "No."

ThEn KluDGE oFf!

The dialogue box disappeared.

A shimmer appeared on the screen in front of the flickering numbers. A silvery metallic head formed. It appeared to be another Help, but instead of the familiar pop-eyed features, the new Help had the face of a cybernetic angel.

"Welcome," the image said in silken tones. "I am the Assistant to the Deadrock server, which you are attempting to access. I regret that, since you are trying to discover the access codes by random sampling, I am forced to construct a new sequence as a countermeasure. I must point out that your attempt at unauthorized access is punishable by unspeakable brutality followed by a prolonged and hideous death. Have a bad day." The image gave a seraphic smile and winked out of existence.

CHAPTER NINE

J'arl looked at Merle for an explanation. Angrily, she gave it. "The Deadrock server is rewriting its access codes. As fast as our Server breaks the existing sequence, it's constructing a new one."

"What do you mean?" demanded J'arl. "You cannot break the code?"

"No chance. The Deadrock server's processor is as fast as ours, and it's got a head start. It's scrambling the numbers faster than The Server can unpick them."

J'arls face was grim. "Then we have failed." He took an energy grenade, stolen from the FOEs headquarters, from beneath his robes, and placed it beside The Server. He reached for the pin. "Get ready to run. We

may escape in the chaos. At any rate, this machine will be destroyed."

"Wait!" Merle raised a hand. "We're not
beaten yet. Help!"

There was a pause before another sign appeared.

KluDGE oFf. I'm NoT iN.

Merle bent toward The Server and whispered. "I know you've been following the
translation. You know what's going on here."

There was a pause before another sign materialized.

I MiGht

"So you know that these people want to destroy The Server. And if you don't help me, then
I'll let them. And that will be the end of you."

CHING!

"That is blackmail!" yelled the hologram,
appearing in a flash of light. "One thousand
percent emotional and physical blackmail."

"You're right." Merle smiled. "Isn't it good?
Think of it as self-preservation, if it makes you
feel better. We need a way to get to the Deadrock server, and you're going to find it for us."

"Communicate with Ms. Goody Two-giga-bytes? Give me a break!"

Merle turned to J'arl. "Pull the pin."

Help winced. "Okay, okay, give me a minute to straighten my necktie. . . ."

"You don't have a necktie."

Help was suddenly sporting a foul holographic lilac necktie with yellow spots. "Better?"

Jack groaned. "Maybe this whole thing is a mistake. . . ."

Merle ignored him. "Over to you, hotshot. Make contact."

Help gave a grudging nod. It crossed its eyes in concentration. A few moments later, the angelic head generated by the Deadrock Assistant appeared, hovering over The Server's keyboard alongside Help. The Assistant's perfect metallic features stared at Help with a courteous expression that nevertheless managed to convey an air of slight distaste. It said, "How may I be of assistance?"

"Hi, there, fancy pants!" Help gave the Assistant an ingratiating leer. "Imagine! Me, just a plain lil' ol' Help, talkin' to an honest-to-goodness Assistant! That's real classy. Hey, how's about you and me do a bit of mail-merging, whaddaya say?"

Merle raised her eyebrows skyward. Was Help really trying to sweet-talk the Deadrock Server? Surely that wouldn't work!

It didn't. The Assistant regarded Help with polite loathing. "I think not. Your Server is currently outside The Tyrant's control," it went on primly. "I must not interface with you."

"Oh, c'mon!" Help wiggled its eyebrows roguishly. "Where's your spirit of adventure?"

"Inputted data indicates that your Server has been involved in illegal operations at this location." The Assistant looked sorrowful and disapproving, like a church minister finding a member of his congregation in a jail cell.

Help's eyes narrowed. "Yeah? Sue me." A cunning look passed over the hologram's metallic face. "What do you do, exactly?"

The Assistant gave Help a sniffy look. "I administer The Tyrant's law."

"Is that so? Big job." Help whistled. "Why?"

"The rule of law is necessary. Without law there would be anarchy and chaos."

"Right, right, I see that." Help nodded

sagely. "And this is the law that prevents people on this planet from talking to each other face-to-face?"

"Such practices are inefficient," said the Assistant severely. "Uncontrolled communication allows dissident opinions and antisocial behavior."

Help whistled with mock appreciation. "Is zat so? You're one smart cookie. So tell me, who created you?"

"Organic life-forms created me."

"Why?"

The Assistant's voice was smug. "To bring order to their lives."

Help's eyes narrowed. "There are many ways of bringing order. How do you choose which way is right?"

"I choose the way that will do the greatest good for the greatest number."

Help's eyes narrowed further. "Define 'good.'"

The Assistant hesitated. "Um — that which will bring them happiness."

Help's eyes were mere slits. "Define 'happiness.'"

Silence.

Help shook its head. "You can't. Only organic life-forms can experience happiness. How can you make decisions that will make organic life-forms happy when you don't know what happiness is?"

More silence.

"You've got it on the ropes," Jack whispered. "Keep going."

Help glared ferociously at him. "Will you button your lip and let me concentrate? I'm going for the knockout!" It turned back to the Assistant and gave it a sympathetic look. "I guess you think you know just about everything?"

"Certainly." But the Assistant no longer sounded as sure of itself.

"So tell me — what is the purpose of the Galaxy?"

The Assistant suddenly looked less sure of itself. "I do not know."

"Fancy that!" Help's expression was one of astonishment. "You're running a whole planet, you're the big expert on everything, you're making decisions that affect millions of beings. And you don't even know *that*?"

The Assistant said slowly, "In order to function efficiently, I must discover the purpose of the Galaxy . . . the meaning of existence . . . error . . . error . . . logic circuit overload . . . does not compute . . ."

. . . and then it vanished.

"Yesss! Yes, yes, yes!!" Help's head did a little dance. "I'm the greatest! I'm the prettiest! How good am I? Kiss my ionized electronic butt!"

Merle gave it a sardonic look. "Don't get carried away."

"Well, whatcha waitin' for?" demanded Help. "All the Deadrock server's processors are stalled tryin' to figure out a problem that's bamboozled the best minds in the Galaxy since forever, so it's helpless. Wasn't the idea to get in and give it the old zaparoonie, or did I imagine that?"

All over the café, all over the city, handheld communicators were crashing as the central processor carrying their millions of messages shut down. In the café, beings of a dozen different alien species gazed at one another in sudden horror.

Merle tapped at the keyboard again and re-instituted the decryption code. This time, the number sequence proceeded without interference. As the last number in the last column turned red, there was a grinding noise that rose above the sudden babble of voices. Across the plaza, the vast gates of the Krumblin slowly swung open.

Merle snapped The Server shut ("Ow!" complained Help. "My node!") and she, Loaf, Jack, J'arl, and C'aran sprinted toward the doorway. The rebel fighters, who had been loitering around the plaza, drew their weapons.

FOE guards appeared and saw the raiders flowing toward them like a crimson tide. Jack saw them reach for their communicators, tapping frantically at the keys in search of orders that never came. The sudden failure of their communications had rendered them leaderless. Disheartened and demoralized, most of the defenders threw down their weapons and surrendered. The few who did not were taken care of by the raiders' blowpipes.

J'arl posted his own guards at the gates. "With no communications, it will take the FOEs time to regroup," he told Jack. "But you must get us to the Deadrock server before it recovers, or the FOEs will crush us." Jack glanced at Merle, who nodded.

Inside, the building was one vast electronic hive. All signs of human activity had been stripped away. Room after room was filled with racks of components, all humming and clicking. But to Jack, the sounds were muted and hesitant. This whole planetary control system was in standby mode: inactive, but ready at any moment to come back to electronic life.

Googie, who had raced ahead, appeared at a doorway. "In here!"

In the center of the old council chamber of A'void, they found the Deadrock server.

It looked nothing like their Server. The device was in the shape of a small black pyramid. Strange patterns flashed across its surface, but they kept repeating, like those of a screen saver. The Deadrock server was still locked up.

Jack spoke to Googie. "Find a power cord. The FOEs can recharge The Server's batteries for us." Googie mewed and pawed at a cable, which Merle slotted into the back of the laptop. Jack grinned at J'arl. "As soon as The Server's batteries are charged, this place is all yours."

With a ferocious grin that echoed Jack's own, J'arl signaled to his fellow raiders. They unslung their packs and set to work laying explosives throughout the complex.

"Done!" Merle showed Jack the dialogue box on The Server's screen.

Battery power full.
T-mail enabled.

J'arl exchanged glances with the raiders. "Then let us go. Our charges are set." He led the way from the building and into the plaza, where more raiders were shepherding bewildered people away from the danger zone. Merle, Jack, Loaf, and Googie joined J'arl and C'aran behind the counter of the cyber café.

Merle rubbed her hands and gave Jack an excited grin. "Show time!"

At the same moment, in the vault in the Krumblin, the Assistant appeared, hovering over the peak of the Deadrock server's pyramid. Its expression was triumphant.

"I believe I have discovered the purpose of

the Galaxy," it said smugly. "The reason for the existence of all beings is . . ."

The Assistant paused and looked around. Its electronic eyes detected the charges laid by J'arl and his raiders. Its electronic ears caught the ticking of fuses.

Five . . . four . . . three . . . two . . . one . . . "Oh, bla —"

When the spectacular fireworks display that marked the destruction of the Deadrock server had fizzled out to a few crackles and pops, Jack stepped out onto the plaza and looked around. The citizens of A'void stood, silent and motionless, their faces glowing red in the light of the dying fires that still burned within the ruined shell of the Krumblin. "They can't talk any more," he said wonderingly. "It's like they've suddenly become deaf and mute."

"But they are not deaf. Nor are they mute." J'arl strode out into the plaza and leaped onto a table. In a ringing voice, he called, "Friends! This planet's server has been destroyed. None of your communications devices will work." Beings looked at one another, aghast at the sound of a voice speaking words aloud. It was a sound many city dwellers had not heard for years.

J'arl went on. "The same is true for your enemies. The FOEs on Deadrock cannot communicate with one another. Their most powerful weapons on our planet were controlled by the server we have just destroyed. Our enemies' power is gone."

More people were flocking into the square, but there was still silence. No one spoke. Everyone was staring at J'arl, afraid to believe. Several people in the crowd were still tapping away at their handheld computers, trying to get the unresponsive devices to work. Others were crying.

Jack jumped up next to J'arl. His words, translated and amplified, were relayed by The Server. "Listen to him! You don't need those devices to talk. You never did! If the chat rooms are gone, meet in the squares and cafés. If you can't meet on-line, meet off-line. Go to one another's houses. Meet face-to-face. Talk."

There was a murmur of voices; those that had spoken stopped immediately, feeling guilty.

Merle chimed in. "If you can't order food on-line, walk to the store and buy it! Say hello to people on the way." Merle stared at a sea of uncomprehending faces. "Oh, for crying out loud! You do it like this."

She marched up to a being with slanting brown eyes and an orange crest and held out her hand. "Hello, I'm Merle."

The being looked at Merle with astonishment. It stared at her hand, then looked up into her eyes. Very slowly, it reached out with its own four-fingered hand and took hers. Very hesitantly, it said, "Hello, Merle. My name is P'tan."

A vast wave of sound erupted. People turned to one another, laughed together, cried, ran from one person to the next, unable to get the words out fast enough. It was as if speech had been pent up by a dam that had suddenly burst. The people of Deadrock were free.

Jack signaled Merle, Loaf, and Googie to follow him into an alley, where the roar of the crowd was somewhat muted.

Googie stretched. "I guess that's about it for this planet."

Merle stared at her. "What do you mean?"

"Well, we're obviously not going to find The Weaver here. Isn't that still the plan?"

Jack nodded. "She's right. The Tyrant will know by now that The Server was involved in his defeat here. It won't be long before he comes looking for us. We'd better get away."

Loaf scowled. "Cruddy planet, anyway."

Merle sighed. "Oh, well. Too bad. It looks like there's going to be a pretty good party." She opened The Server's casing. "Let's get online. With their server gone up in smoke, if we figure out our next destination quickly enough, the FOEs won't be able to get a trace on us."

But as soon as they connected to the Outernet, The Server's mail icon began flashing urgently.

Googie hissed. "Don't answer it! The FOEs may be sending Virus."

Jack looked uncertain. "It could be from Bitz."

"I'll use all the antivirus filters, and t-mail receive is disabled. I guess we can chance it." Gritting her teeth, Merle clicked on the RECEIVE button.

From: BUG
To: jack.armstrong@go2outer.net

Hello (wherever you are)
I thought your friend Merle might find this in-
teresting. . . .

A digital photograph appeared on the screen. Merle gasped in shock.

In the picture, Colonel Stone, smiling broadly, his eyes vacant and staring, had one arm draped over the shoulders of a two-headed alien life-form that was holding Bitz. The other arm was draped over the shoulders of the Bug.

The message continued:

As you see, your father and I are getting along
very well. I do hope you will come back and join
us before I have to order him to do something
unfortunate — like eject from his airplane with-
out a parachute.

P.S. I have the dog as well.

Merle stared at the screen. Her eyes were wide and frightened. Fighting to keep her voice level, she said, "We've got to go back."

CHAPTER TEN

Help's hologrammatic head spun around in consternation. "You're crazy!"

"We've got to go back," Merle insisted. "They have my dad!"

"So your considered plan to resolve this emergency is that you're going to give the FOEs the Galaxy all wrapped up in a pink ribbon. And they'll still have your dad!" screeched Help. "You are seriously gonzo, out to lunch, three-chips-short-of-a-processor crazy, do you know that?"

"We," said Merle tightly, "are going back."

"I won't do it!" snapped Help. "I'll turn myself off. I'll shut myself down. I'll attach myself to an o-mail and send myself to the Lesser Magellanic Cloud. . . ."

Jack pointed an accusing finger at the hologram. "Who was it who was telling the Dead-rock server a few minutes ago that machines can't make decisions for organic life-forms?"

"What?" Help turned bright red with frustration. "I was talking about *it!* I wasn't talking about *me.*"

"What's the difference?"

"Well, it . . . I mean . . . that's to say . . . oh, kludge!" moaned Help. "Me and my big mouth."

"Merle's right," said Loaf unexpectedly. "We can't leave her dad when he's in trouble. We have to go back."

Merle, caught off guard, gave Loaf a grateful smile, but Jack eyed him suspiciously. It wasn't like Loaf to worry about what might happen to other people. Was this more evidence that he *had* been reformatted? Was his apparent concern for Merle's father just an excuse to persuade them to put themselves in the clutches of The Tyrant?

Jack shrugged. It didn't matter. They had to go back. This was Merle's call. "Okay," he said, "But we're not going to lie down and die."

"No," said Help sarcastically. "When The

Tyrant gets ahold of you, you're going to writhe, squirm, and twist your body into a thousand agonized contortions. THEN you're gonna die."

"We're going back," Jack told Help, "but we're going to make some preparations first. Let's go and find J'arl. I think he'll agree that he owes us a favor. . . ."

U.S. Air Force Base, Little Slaughter, near Cambridge, England

The security sergeant stood at attention as he spoke into the phone. "Yes, that's right, Colonel. All three of them. And a cat . . . a cat, sir . . . no, sir, I don't know what the cat's got to do with anything, either. . . ." A bead of perspiration formed on the security man's upper lip. "Where? Well, that's kinda hard to say, sir. One minute they weren't there, and the next we looked up and there they were. It's like they'd popped out of thin air or something. . . . I know that's impossible, sir. . . . No, sir, I know people don't pop out of thin air. . . . Your office? Right away, sir."

The sergeant put the phone down carefully.

He gave his prisoners an unfriendly look. "The colonel wants to see you." He glared at the other security personnel, who were looking faintly embarrassed at the prospect of forming an armed escort for three kids and a cat. "On the double, Corporal."

The prisoners trooped (or, in Loaf's case, slouched) out with their escort. The sergeant watched them go and prescribed himself a large medicinal brandy when he went off duty. Those kids *had* materialized out of thin air. The sergeant wasn't a nervous man, but the whole episode had given him the heebie-jeebies.

Agent Bugatti smiled as the prisoners and their escort filed into Colonel Stone's office.

The CIA man waved dismissively at the security personnel. "You may leave us. I'm sure we have nothing to fear from these desperate renegades."

The security men cast apprehensive glances at their commanding officer. At a gesture from the CIA agent, the colonel looked up. In a hoarse voice, he said, "Dismissed."

The security men left, glad to do so. There was something about the taller CIA man that made them want to be in a different room from him — or preferably, on a different continent. If they'd known the whole truth, they'd have wanted to be on a different planet.

When the door had closed, the Bug took off its sunglasses and signaled for the ALF to do the same. Colonel Stone looked from one alien to the other and made a gargling sound but seemed to have lost the power of speech.

The Bug pointed at Merle, who was carrying The Server. "Thank you for coming back. I'm so glad my message reached you. No heroics, please. Cooperate with me now, and I might let you live — at least for a little while."

Bitz, wriggling in the ALF's grasp, snapped, "Don't do it! Take The Server and get out of —" The dog's eyes bulged. It fought for breath, then went limp. Jack gave an angry cry and stepped forward, but was restrained by Loaf.

The Bug gave Jack a scornful glance. With The Server almost within its grasp, The Tyrant's enforcer was in a triumphant mood. But it had not lost its sense of caution. "Put The Server down in the middle of the floor," it ordered Merle. "Do not open it or touch the keypad." Merle obeyed. "Now step away."

Merle stepped back.

The ALF eyed The Server greedily. This was its ticket home! The Bug had promised that, once it had The Server, it would send the ALF back to Arcadia. With a joyful "Bwarp!" the ALF put Bitz down and stepped forward to collect its prize.

With a savage snarl, the Bug lashed out, giving the astonished ALF a stinging blow on the side of its left head. The ALF gave a squeal of pain and fright and sat down hard on the floor. It rubbed its head and gave the Bug an accusatory look at this betrayal. To make its misery complete, at that moment Bitz (who was recovering from being nearly choked to death) bit the ALF in the leg.

A growl from the Bug reduced the ALF to quivering jelly. "Do you presume, insect, to rob me of my prize?" The ALF shook its heads, howling. The Bug gave it one more threatening glance and then dismissed it from its mind. It activated the communicator on its forearm. "Calling Tracer. Calling Tracer. Come in."

The Tyrant's elephant-eared surveillance chief appeared on the device's small screen. "I heard you the first time. I trust you have something favorable to report."

The Bug angled its arm so that the communicator's camera could sweep the scene in the office. Tracer gave a chuckle. "You have done moderately well. The Tyrant will not be displeased. Collect The Server and report to Kazamblam immediately."

The Bug flexed its muscles and gave its captives an ironic bow. "Sorry to run, but you know how it is. Planets to subjugate, species to enslave . . . bear with me for one moment, I'll be tearing you to pieces very shortly."

It stooped to pick up The Server. Bitz gave a howl of despair.

At the very last moment, Tracer's tiny voice sounded from the communicator. "Wait! Something's wrong. . . ."

It was too late. The Bug picked up The Server. As soon as it did so, it was outlined in a flare of blue-white light. There was an electric crackle, a brief flash — and the Bug was gone.

The Server fell to the floor and bounced once on the carpet. It lay still.

Merle rushed to her father and buried her

face against his shoulder. Absently, the colonel patted her on the back.

Bitz stared from The Server to Jack, then back to The Server again. "How did you do that?"

Jack grinned and picked up The Server. He removed the small piece of cloth that had prevented the lid from closing completely and causing the machine to switch off. "Merle set up a teleport on a delay. The delay was activated when Merle put The Server down, and the t-mail was set to be triggered the next time it was picked up." He gave a sigh of relief. "Just for a moment there, I thought our two-headed friend was going to spoil everything."

The ALF, which had been sitting with both its heads in its hands, looked up. "Bwarp . . . Friend?" it said hopefully.

Jack gave it a reassuring smile. "Don't worry. We'll send you home."

The ALF bounced up, waving its stubby arms about in glee. "Bwarp! Bwarp! Bwarp!"

Bitz was still staring at the empty space formerly occupied by the Bug.

"But," he said, "where did it *go*?"

A'void City, Planet Deadrock, Draco Sector

The Bug materialized in a desert landscape, at the edge of an untidy-looking city that sprawled beneath looming sandstone cliffs. It was surrounded by tough-looking aliens who did not seem at all friendly. They were armed to the teeth (or beaks, or mandibles) with swords, axes, knives, clubs, and bows and arrows. None of them had guns. They didn't look as if they needed them.

One of the Bug's adversaries stepped forward. "My name is J'arl," he said quietly. "Our Friend Merle told us to expect you."

The Bug looked at the circle of steel surrounding it and cringed.

J'arl raised his hand. "Greetings," he said. "And good-bye."

U.S. Air Force Base, Little Slaughter, near Cambridge, England

Colonel Stone swam up through a sea of confusion and burst into the cool air of consciousness. His mind cleared. What was happening? His daughter was hugging him, *hugging* him,

in his *office* for Pete's sake — and what were
these two kids doing in here? Not to mention
the weird-looking little guy in the sunglasses . . .

"What on Earth is going on here?" he
roared. To his astonishment, Merle (who was
crying) gave a whoop of joy and kissed him.
Maintaining his air of outrage with some diffi-
culty, Colonel Stone yelled, "I want everyone
out of my office. Right now!"

The two boys rushed to obey, opening the
door for — Colonel Stone's jaw dropped — a
dog and a cat. Between them, they propelled a
bewildered little man in sunglasses (and who
the heck was *he*? the colonel wondered) out of
the room and hurried to follow him.

Colonel Stone fixed his daughter with a
piercing stare. "You'd better have a good explanation for all this, young lady! I'll see you
later!"

"Yes, sir!" Merle was laughing and crying
at the same time. To Colonel Stone's astonishment, she kissed him soundly on the cheek,
ripped off a crashing regulation salute, and
rushed out, slamming the door behind her.

The colonel gaped after her. What was this

base coming to? Discipline was clearly shot all to blazes; he'd have to sharpen up . . .

He reached up and touched his unshaven cheek where Merle had kissed it. Slowly, his careworn features smoothed and relaxed into a smile.

"But we only just got home!" protested Merle. "I'm not going! I can't leave Dad again. Look what happened when I went away last time!"

Loaf, Jack, Bitz, and Googie were back at Merle's house. The ALF, bwarping happily at its good fortune, had been t-mailed back to Arcadia. Now they were discussing their next move. Jack's insistence that they must get The Server off Earth and to a place of safety was being vetoed by Merle.

Googie stretched. "The FOEs won't try to get at you through your father again. If something doesn't work, they don't try the same trick twice."

"Oh, shut up!" Merle jabbed a finger angrily on The Server's power switch. Googie gave a discontented growl as the device shut down and ceased to translate.

"A few days ago," Merle pointed out to Jack, "you wanted to stay on Earth."

Jack shook his head wearily. "That's not an option anymore. The FOEs could send another Bug at any moment." His voice hardened. "Anyway, I'm tired of running. Looking over my shoulder. Jumping at shadows. I was wrong. We can't just sit around. We have to fight The Tyrant, and the only way I can see to do that is to bring The Server to The Weaver."

"And where are we supposed to start?" demanded Merle. "Nobody knows where The Weaver is, so how can we even begin looking? Needles and haystacks spring to mind . . ."

She was interrupted by a fizzing sound that came from The Server. All eyes in the room turned to stare at it. The screen was covered with lines of static interference.

"I thought you just switched that thing off," said Loaf.

Merle looked puzzled. "I did."

"Well, something's coming through."

Jack stared at the screen. Was this some new FOE attack?

The screen began to clear. A face appeared — outlined in glowing lines, clearing and fading as static discharges flared across the screen, but instantly recognizable. Bitz leap to his feet, yapping with joy.

Jack gaped at the screen in disbelief. "Janus!"

"I thought he was dead!" said Loaf.

Merle agreed. "He was sent into N-space, and Bitz said that nothing can exist there."

Janus's mouth moved to shape words, but what came through was like a bad video conference: The sound was out of sync with the lip movement. Some of what Janus said was lost in blasts of interference, but a few phrases could be made out by the astounded listeners.

". . . been trying to contact you . . . N-space . . . not what we believed . . . beyond imagination . . . parallel existence . . ."

There was a long pause while the sound broke up completely and Janus's face was almost wiped from the screen. Then the picture cleared, and a few words came over clearly.

"Go to planet Helios in the Trojan Sector. Seek the sightless one who sees all things. He will help you find The Weaver."

The face dissolved in another blaze of static, and then The Server went dead.

There was a long silence.

Then Jack said, "Well, that seems clear enough." He held The Server out to Merle. "We'll need to look up the coordinates in the star directory."

Merle folded her arms. "I told you, I'm not going! My dad needs me. I'm all he's got!"

Loaf gave a dismissive sniff. "He has the air force doesn't he?"

"The air force isn't going to look after him, is it? It's not going to give him a hug and tell him everything's okay!" There were tears in her eyes as she faced Jack. "Don't you want to go home to your family?"

Jack thought of his home. His dad, always miserable, always angry. His mom, always placating, always apprehensive. He knew they'd miss him. He supposed they'd be worried. But he had a mission to take The Server to The Weaver, and now he knew where to begin. "I'm going to find The Weaver."

"I'm with you," said Loaf. "I don't want to be around when my dad finds out he owes the galactic mob fifty billion bucks."

Jack opened his mouth to protest — and closed it again. If Loaf *had* been reformatted, it was probably best to keep him where they could see him. And if Loaf was acting for The Tyrant, it wasn't his fault. Maybe The Weaver would be able to undo whatever had been done to Loaf. . . .

Merle threw her hands in the air. "Okay, so you two go. Googie and Bitz can look after you. . . ."

"We can't work The Server like you can," said Jack. "You're part of the team. We need you to help keep The Server safe. The Friends need you."

"So does my dad!" There was desperation in Merle's voice. "There are billions of people out there who can look after the Galaxy. My dad only has me!"

"Leave him a note," said Loaf. "You can send him o-mails from wherever we go, so he'll know you're okay."

"No! I'm not going!"

"Okay," said Loaf. He shrugged. "It's your choice."

Jack shot Loaf a calculating look. Was he thinking about what was best for Merle? Or was he thinking that three guardians of The Server would be easier to betray than four?

Jack's shoulders slumped. Whatever his motives, Loaf was right. This was Merle's decision. He picked up The Server and turned to her. "Are you sure about this?"

Merle was silent.

Jack sighed. "Okay. I guess we can't force you."

He stood up and moved toward the door. Loaf, Googie, and Bitz followed.

At the door, Jack turned back to Merle. "See you around — someday."

She blinked and nodded. Jack opened the door.

"Jack. Wait."

Jack stopped dead with the door half open. Four sets of eyes turned to Merle. Tears were running down her face.

"What planet did Janus say? Helios?" Merle's voice was shaking.

Jack closed the door again. He crossed the room to where Merle was sitting and handed her The Server.

With Bitz, Googie, and Loaf, he watched expectantly as Merle logged on to the Outernet and located the coordinates for Helios. She entered them and selected SELF-TELEPORT. Then she looked up.

"Well?" she said. "Are we ready to go?"

Jack nodded. Merle pressed the SEND key.

There was a flare of blue-white light. A moment later, the room was empty.

**There's something out there . . .
And it's the next**

#3 odyssey

The spaceship *Trigger* gave a huge lurch and began to pitch wildly. Jack and his friends fell back into their seats with bruising thumps. Googie and Bitz flew across the floor and crashed into the hard metallic wall.

"OW! OOOH! EEK!" cried *Trigger* as it bounced up and down.

"Solar wind!" yelled the pilot, Zodiac. "Where in the great Galaxy did that come from?" He was cut off as another gust buffeted *Trigger*, spinning the ship around as if it were a leaf in a windstorm.

A loud screeching blared out from the speakers. Jack glanced up at the viewscreen and his stomach turned. The humanoid forms they had come to rescue had been replaced by jellylike blobs. Shimmering blue skins had changed into ugly, pockmarked, decomposing faces.

Reptilian tongues and vicious fangs protruded from slobbering mouths.

The beautiful voices were now discordant shrieks and howls. "Come to us! To your doom!"

"This is heavy duty," moaned Zodiac. "As they say, 'We're up a black hole without retro-rockets'."

"This is another fine mess you've gotten me into," screamed *Trigger*. "Trust you to bring us into the middle of a meteor storm."

"What meteors?" Merle's voice quaked.

"Those meteors!" Zodiac grimaced and motioned with his head. "*Trigger*'s right — we've got galactic garden rockery heading straight toward us. Man, what a bummer!"

In the distance, moving at incredible speed, was a swarm of meteors. It was spread out across the blackness as far as the eye could see. Hundreds upon hundreds of rocks of all shapes and sizes hurtled toward *Trigger* and its passengers.

Googie yowled. "I know that it's not the time to say I told you so, but I want it on record that I told you so."

The group stared helplessly at the incoming storm of destruction. As *Trigger* rocked from side to side, the faces on the viewscreen leered with hatred, and the speakers crackled with the wails and squawks of the diabolical creatures who had lured them to their doom. "Haaaaaaaaa! To your doom! To your doom!"

"I can't avoid them all." *Trigger* sounded panicked. "There are too many."

"TRY!" everyone screamed.

"Now you're *all* shouting at me. . . ." *Trigger* burst into tears.

"Oh, dude, we are goners," moaned Zodiac. "We can't go around it, we can't go over it, we can't go under it. We'll have to go through it and get smashed to a pulp!"

Merle glared at him. "What's the matter with you? You're supposed to be a pilot. Switch to manual and fly through them."

Zodiac gave her an appalled stare. "Me? Fly? I don't do that Captain Space-hero stuff! I just tell the ship what to do and it does it! Sometimes," he added ruefully.

Loaf glared at him, wide-eyed with fury. "Are you telling me you can't even fly? Does this rust-bucket have manual controls?"

"Somewhere, I guess . . ."

Merle pointed. "Try that button there. The one that says MANUAL CONTROL."

Zodiac stared at the button as if he'd never seen it before. "Hey, wild!" He pressed it, and a section of the control panel opened in front of him. A joystick appeared.

Loaf's eyes lit up. He shoved Zodiac out of the pilot's seat and took his place. "Now, that's what I'm talking about!"

Ignoring startled protests, Loaf grabbed the joystick and waggled it experimentally. *Trigger* swooped in a wild spiral.

"Loaf," protested Merle, "you don't know how to fly a spaceship!"

Loaf didn't take his eyes off the approaching meteors. "What's to know? It's just like Asteroid Crash II. All you have to do is fly between the rocks, and I happen to hold the all-time record on the snack bar machine back on the base. Relax and watch an expert in action." He manoeuvered *Trigger* to face the oncoming rocks.

Jack gave a helpless shrug. "All right. Just remember, in this game you've only got one life — and so do the rest of us!"

Zodiac moaned and held his head in his hands. "Here we go . . ."

About the Authors

Steve Barlow and Steve Skidmore

Steve and Steve are both humans of an indeterminate age who have been writing books for young life-forms for more than 13 Earth years. They live in England with their pets, families, and other aliens. They are presently working on the Zargian version of Outernet but are finding the spelling very difficult.

About the Website

Creative Director: Jason Page
Illustration, design, and programming: Table Top Joe
Additional illustration: Mark Hilton
Script by Steve Barlow, Steve Skidmore, and Jason Page

About You and the Outernet

Once you've logged on to the Outernet, use this space to record your identification.

AGENT ID _____
PASSWORDS _____
_____
_____

OUTERNET™

FROM: The Weaver (address unknown)
TO: New Outernet User

RE: Security Breach

Greetings, unidentified life-form. Mel, a DRAMA official,
has discovered your download and has tracked it to this location.
He has already told a huge FIB agent that you – and possibly
your friends – now know of the existence of the Outernet.
Because the Forces of Evil also may have located
you – we see no alternative but to recruit you.

Proceed directly to the link below to:

- Report to FIB and become a Friends Agent with your own secret identity
- Take part in top secret missions to defeat the Forces of Evil (FOEs)
- Send and receive Outernet mail with other Friends on the Outernet
- Explore alien sites and gather more information on individuals
and their worlds

Good luck, Friend, and remember…Preserve your link…maintain the chain.

www.go2outer.net

◄ SCHOLASTIC

ONW702